A Mouse in the Vinaigrette.

Helen Ducal.

Helen Ducal has asserted her right under the Copyright, design, and Patents Act 1988 to be identified as the author of this work.

Copyright © 2012 Helen Ducal

Also by Helen Ducal.

All Expenses Paid (fact meets fiction)

Granny sitting in the south of France.

Shelf Life. Everybody has one. Would you want to know yours?

Khamaileon. A maternity suit and even DNA cannot help her.

MISSING? A 3 yr old girl writes her autobiography from 6 feet under.

Mature, educated, healing hands, can travel. Book 1.

Samantha Wilde, estate agent by day, escort by night.

<u>All available on Amazon kindle.</u>

Works in Progress.

Wait for Me. Two souls. Six Lives.

Decree Absolutely. You keep the house (and develop a thriving business)

Souvenir. A play without words. Music from 1950's to 1990's tell the story.

Parallel Lives. Two iconoclasts tell their story. Madonna and Colette.

Not Always. Abuse begets abuse…not always.

A knock at the door. Treated for the wrong complaint.

My dreams and other stories. Short stories.

7 Steps to Paradise. Southampton to the south of France.

A funny thing happened. My life so far.

A Carer's Survival Guide.

25 years as a live-in carer. All you need to know…and somethings you wish you didn't**.**

 Letting Go of Grace. The link between twin sisters goes further back that anyone would ever guess.

This book is fiction, except the parts based on facts.

My good friend, Laura Bennett has had a very interesting life so far.

Here are some more of her stories.

She prefers this title.

You don't pay me enough. Get Me Out of Here.

Introduction:

No humans, not even men, or animals, even mice, were harmed during the making of this book.

****

Be sure of one thing. If you take a job as a live-in carer/housekeeper/cook, you will be privy to many a tale of the unexpected. But you will never be bored.

At least, this is what you tell yourself when you start crossing off the days until you leave, on the kitchen calendar, just like a hostage...

For Kate.

You would love it here.

There is so much sky.

Chapters

1. If the agency had sent a photo, I would have asked them not to send you.
2. Stepford Wives are alive and well on the Riviera.
3. Miss Babs.
4. Don't open any windows. All the frames are rotten.
5. Hat, scarf, gloves, goodnight.
6. Helpful friends. Stop her meds, she'll be dead in about 10 days.
7. You sure you know what you are doing with that syringe?
8. You look whacked. Go and lie down, I'll bring you a cup of tea.
9. A Mouse in the Vinaigrette
10. Midnight chocolate nibbler
11. The Spirit of Christmas
12. Taps and tackle.
13. A Vision in White.
14. Hove, actually.
15. Just tell him, goodbye.
16. Phone your mother. Tell her, you are getting married next week.
17. I had the bathroom re-tiled after my son shot himself in there.
18. We're off home now. Thank you for having us.
19. Short term memory. Nil.
20. Sherry by street light.
21. Just Winifred.
22. Rose.
23. Pets: Brandy.
24. Pets: Rosie the golden retriever
25. Work for a celebrity.
26. Vignettes.

1. If the agency had sent a photo, I would have asked them not to send you.

Not exactly what you want to hear after a flight from Heathrow to Rome and not to mention a hair-raising twenty minute journey with a taxi driver that swerved at every given opportunity, and even some imaginary ones.

The job description given by the agency had been too good to be true.

It went like this.

53 year old American lady wishes to find housekeeper/cook/driver/PA for a property in the South of France.

My hand had gone up, involuntarily. Bit pointless as we were on the phone at the time.

(This was long before Skype)

"I'll do it. Where exactly is it, the property, I mean?" I had asked.

I was thinking, St Tropez, Monte Carlo...

"That's the part you are really going to love, Laura," cooed Christine, my soon to be despised, companion co-ordinator, at Bla, Bla, agency.

"The lady in question, is currently in Rome and would like you to meet her there, then fly to Nice where you will hire a car to start your property search."

I thought I had died and gone to heaven. I was going to drive round the south of France, poking my nose into posh people's homes and get paid for it.

Tip #1 You can never have too much information about a job.

I felt my other hand go up, in case my enthusiasm had gone unnoticed.

I was still on the phone and now hands free as I danced around the room.

"So, what do you say?" Asked Christine, trying to keep the smugness out of her voice.

"I'll do it. When do I start?"

It was 2.15p.m on a very damp, grey, English, Tuesday afternoon in March.

"Oh good. You're booked on the 15.15 from Heathrow to Rome, tomorrow."

"Wow, it's a good job I accepted then."

"I haven't known you long but I thought this was right up your street."

"Sounds amazing. So just before I let the adrenaline completely take over, what's the... but?"

"Well there isn't one really. Oh, you don't mind dogs, do you? You've looked after clients with dogs before."

 Slight note of panic in the voice there.

Too good to resist.

"Ah well. Hum. I don't know. What kind of dog?"

I heard rustling of papers.

"A Shih tzu. It's only small. Goes everywhere with her, even in the plane."

She winced.

"Oh boy. You weren't going to tell me, were you?"

"Sorry, slipped my mind. I do have a lot of clients, you know."

"Okay, okay. I'll do it but then you obviously knew that when you booked the ticket."

"Rome for three days, then Nice to search for a villa. Listen, if you don't go, I will."

***

So flipping convincing, she was. I wasn't in the habit of visiting the plush London offices of Bla-di-Bla and Co but when I got back from this, I would make an exception.

Villa Delparco was a small but beautifully formed hotel. Right in the heart of Rome. Probably. I actually had no idea where I was. With the time difference, the flight and the taxi ride, it was now 8 p.m. local time.

I sauntered up to the reception desk, trying to look as though I belonged there, all the time eyeing the fabulous display of anti-pasto, peeking out of the entrance to the restaurant.

I was starving.

"Buona sera. Il mio nome è Miss Bennett. Sono qui per...

I had been practising in the taxi and then suddenly I forgot the client's name.

"Ah yes, Miss Bennett, you are here as a guest of Miss Cohen."

He spoke perfect English and his accent was nearly as delicious as the parma ham that had been sliced and arranged to look like the tail feathers of an enormous bird.

"Yes. I am."

"She said I should send you straight to her room, when you arrived."

I glanced back at the entrance to the restuarant.

Giovanni, his name was on his lapel, smiled and added.

"Miss Cohen often has meals in her room."

He either looked sad or disapproving or both it was hard to say. The dark pools that were substituting for eyes had me locked in. The six o clock shadow lurking round his dimpled chin and perfect mouth did little to bring me back to my senses.

"Perhaps she may come down, now you are here."

A perfectly sensible suggestion which somehow converted in my brain, to mean. She can eat down here and you can come to my room...

If Giovanni was reading my thoughts I was in big trouble.

He handed me my key. 601.

Miss Cohen was to be found next door in 603.

I soon discovered that 666 might have been more appropriate.

I knocked tentatively on the door of 603.

There was no reply. In the bathroom, maybe? I knocked again.

Giovanni smiled as he walked past with my suitcase. I handed him my key.

Subtle. Of course he had a pass key, which he waved at me.

He deposited my case and shut my door, then came and stood by me.

"Let me," he offered.

"Miss Cohen.It's Giovanni. Madame, the nice lady from London is here. Shall I open the door?"

Still nothing but Giovanni seemed to hear something. Sounded like a growl.

Uh-oh. The small dog.

Giovanni knocked once more, then turned the handle.

Before I could thank him, he was gone.

American, female, never married, degree in art history, speaks five languages, lived in Japan for three years, dotes on her dog.

What the agency, ---I was going to kill Christine --- hadn't mentioned was that Miss Cohen was an alcoholic, chain smoking, manic depressive with suicidal tendancies.

Funny that.

"You?" Miss Cohen, pointed at me. "They sent you?"

"The agency, yes. I've just arrived from London. My name is..."

"I know who you are. I should have insisted on a photograph."

The last bit was mumbled.

I asked her to repeat it.

She was finding some composure.

" If the agncey."

She spoke as if every word were being weighed and was therefore a great burden.

"If they had sent a photograph. I would have asked them not to send you."

At this point Miss Cohen stubbed out her cigarette into the already overflowing, green onyx ashtray that was precariously sitting in the middle of her double bed.

Just next to the ashtray was Mitsy the shitzu. (my spelling)

They both eyed me with great suspicion.

At least I think they did, it was hard to see through the thick smoke that hung in the room like fog on a November morning in Essex.

"Oh, I'm sorry why is that?"

What else can one say to such a greeting?

"We can have nothing in common," she stated flatly.

Then, as if that made everything okay.

"You're pretty."

I frowned, not sure why this was a crime.

"My father told me when I was eight years old, no man will ever want you for anything but your money, you're ugly."

Good grief. Do the job myself. Would you Christine? Would you?

In my enthusiasm I had neglected to ask if Miss-chain-smoker was a new client?

I was keen to extend the benefit of doubt, for now.

"I studied architecture for two years before going into business on my own." I added helpfully.

Well. I had been married to an architect, I watched him study and I ran a hair and beauty salon. Details...

Miss Cohen started to talk but had a coughing fit instead. I looked around, as best I could, for a glass of water. There was a bottle of Pelligrino in an ice bucket on the dressing table. All the ice had melted and the bottle felt tepid.

I handed her a glass of bubbly water.

She took the smallest sip then handed the glass back to me.

She surprised me by suddenly asking. "Have you eaten?"

"No, I've just..."

She raised her right hand, reaching for her cigarette packet with her left.

"Go," she waved at me. "Down to the restaurant, order whatever you want. They will put it on my account. Then go to bed or go out, I don't care. I don't want to see you. I will call you in the morning. Goodnight."

I stared at the tiny woman, sitting crossed legged in the middle of a double bed. A female version of Woody Allen, shrouded in a grey lightweight, long sleeved, wool shapeless dress, and black tights. Her shoes, reminded me of my school sandals, had been kicked off and were on the floor. She wore oval metal rimmed glasses, which she peered over rather than looked through. Her hair was steely grey and cut into a severe, Mary Quant bob. Her fringe was long enough to touch her glasses. A less confident woman, I had never met.

Miss Cohen could not have been any further from the person I had imagined I would meet, however hard I tried.

I quickly freshened up, in my room, which happily was smoke free. There was a welcoming basket of fruit and an ice bucket with small bottles of mineral water. Some wedges of watermelon had been placed amongst the bottles. As lovely as it looked, I was hungry in a carnivorous way.

When I got downstairs, the restaurant was in full swing and Giovanni was nowhere to be seen. A very prim looking, probably very near retirement age, woman was behind the desk. Her hair was scooped up into a severe bun. She wore huge topaz stone earrings. Her black lace blouse seemed to be multi layered. She looked more Spanish than Italian.

I opened my mouth but she merely nodded and pointed towards the restaurant.

On the one hand if Miss Cohen was going to return me to sender tomorrow I might as well do as she said. *Have whatever you want.* Shame I don't like champagne...not that I would ever do that. But, if by tomorrow morning I suddenly seemed more suitable, maybe I should show a little restraint.

Antipasto to die for, including artichokes, sundried tomatoes, various olives, hams, salamais and on it went. Veal in a delicious lemon sauce with pasta, naturally, followed by zabaione and decaffeinated coffee.

My bed had been turned down and I was ready for sleep but the anticipation I had felt before I arrived was nothing compared to the mixed feelings I had right now. There were going to be a lot of questions asked tomorrow...

I managed to fall asleep somewhere in between the sounds of sirens and high pitched scooters. Definitely Rome.

The phone at the side of my bed gave an intermittent shrill, single note, ring.

I sleepily wondered what good morning was in Italian,but why bother when my charge (ha!) was American and most of the staff spoke English.

"Hello." I volunteered.

" You are booked on a coach trip to the Colosseum, leaving at 10 a.m."

"I'm sorry?"

An irritated sigh, then. "I said, you are..."

"Yes, sorry er, Miss Cohen. I did hear what..."

" Have you had breakfast?"

I glanced at my travel clock. 7.15 a.m.

"Well, no I just..."

"Ring 0 and they will bring it to your room. I will see you back here at 3.30p.m. Then we will decide what is to be done."

She hung up.

The very last thing I felt like doing was getting into a coach with a load of strangers and going to the one place in Rome that I wasn't interested in. Architecture, yes. Gruesome history, no thanks.

I thought about explaining to the tour guide, who would surely speak English, that I had changed my mind and no refund was required.

Then at least I could phone the agency and see some of the Italian capital that didn't resonate with lions and man's inhumanity to man.

I always think there is something wonderfully decadent about room service. I can't resist it, especially when someone else is paying.

Fresh fruit, yoghurt and pastries, washed down with pineapple juice and rot-your-socks, coffee. I was ready for the fray. With my pocket size, Essential Guide to Rome, I had until 3p.m. or thereabouts. What I hadn't bargained for was Miss cough-a-lot being in Reception as the coach arrived to collect any visitors lucky enough to be going on the history tour. Yay!

I wanted this job, I didn't want this job. Decision time. It would seem impolite to refuse this prepaid trip if I were going to have any chance of securing 'my dream job', wouldn't it? I mean, she could stick her cigarette out of the window whenever I was driving her anywhere and we only had two nights in Rome before flying across to Nice. I try never to fall at the first hurdle, so I boarded the coach and waved appreciatively at Miss Cohen who merely gripped Mitsy, who was struggling to break free, even tighter to her side. Carrying the mutt, I would soon find out was, part of the job description.

I persuaded the multi-lingual tour guide that I had been booked on this excursion by mistake. She nodded, then crossed me off her list, three pages long, attached to a clipboard. I ventured the idea that I could rejoin the coach on its return trip to the hotel. She gave me her best, are you serious, look? Perhaps not. I would just have to make sure I returned at the same time and hope Miss Cohen wasn't watching.

Just as every human being has its own unique DNA, apart from identical twins, every client is different. Let me count the ways...

Miss Cohen took me to a whole new realm. Fabulously wealthy. Check. Done that. More than one ailment. Yep, plenty of those. No real friends. Unusual but with others it had seemed by choice, Miss Cohen was one very lonely lady. She telephones her ninety year old father in New York, who is still practising law, at anytime of day or night, to ask incredibly mundane questions. A first. He can be heard screaming at her down the line. Usually in reference to the fact that it is 2a.m. and no, he has no idea whether she should order take-out or risk finding a taxi, in the rain.

Miss Cohen was nowhere in sight when I returned.

But Giovanni was back on duty behind the desk.

"Signora Bennett." He smiled.

I can see so many questions running through his head.

I have one or two of my own but he spoke first.

"She is one unhappy lady." He said solemnly.

That makes two of us, I muttered, not intending him to hear.

"Scusi?"

Ooh. He looks even more Italian today. Unusually tall but dark and handsome as per recommended in all the guide books.

"She was on the phone to London for nearly an hour."

He looked at me, gravely.

I thanked him for the tip off and pressed the button for the lift. I glanced back at him and he sighs, lifting both hands into the air, palms upwards, and mouthing, good luck.

The agency could not replace me for at least a week and strongly recommended that Miss Cohen, give me a try.

This was the gist of the scrawled message, written by Miss Cohen that had been pushed under my door. Interestingly, no one had bothered to ask me , if I wanted to stay?

Then again, I was in Rome and about to go to Nice. How bad could it be?

True to form, Miss-cough-a-lot, had ordered food to be sent to her room. There was a pile of half eaten pasta on a white oval plate. The tray was on the floor and Mitsy was hoovering some miniscule crumbs.

"So," I began, after knocking and entering her bedroom without waiting for a reply. "We'll give it a week then."

I had decided on the, me nanny, you naughty child routine. It was worth a try. Poor old, (ten years older than me) Miss Cohen was a sight to behold. Her hair looked as if it had not been combed in twenty four hours and as far as I could tell she was wearing the same clothes. I really didn't have experience with a client like this, so it would have to be instinct. Fair but firm, I reckoned. Her and the dog.

I managed to see a little more of Rome before we left. Celia, (I was now allowed to her call her this) had seen it all before and did not want to accompany me. The short flight from Rome to Nice sent Mitsy (in her carry-on bag) into a frenzy. She shook for the whole journey. Her owner wasn't much better either. Celia had taken an extra tranquillizer before we left Rome. She was afraid of flying and absolutely not allowed to drink alcohol.

She had phoned ahead to our next hotel to make sure her mini bar was emptied before her arrival.

She did at least try to deal with her demons. I was beginning to feel sorry for her and wondered how on earth, an obviously, extremely intelligent, wealthy woman had become such a wreck. Sorry but there can be no other word for her. I wasn't empathising at this stage, but I was working on it. She certainly tested my patience.

At Nice airport I went to collect the hire car and drove round to arrivals to pick up my charges. (There was only one terminal back then and the airport complex, a lot less...complex). Mitsy had stopped shaking and Celia almost managed a smile. Our next stop was the magnificent hotel on the top of medieval Haute de Cagnes. It wasn't just 5* it was sublime. Celia had booked us a suite each. The view was breathtaking, all the way down to the sea, about five kilometres away and about a fifty minute walk. Celia's smile evaporated at once.

"But I want to be able to walk to the sea!" She looked accusingly at (Giovanni's brother?) as he guided us onto Celia's balcony.

Luckily I had nothing to do with the booking. Celia had simply booked the most expensive hotel she could find that retained an air of seclusion. The Negressco on the Promenade d'Anglais was not her style at all.

We stayed two nights. *The Riviera isn't what it used to be.* So says Celia and off we go. I drove and Celia hung her cigarette hand out of the passenger window. This time we were headed to Toulouse. Much more civilised, she hoped. About halfway through our journey Celia decided to open her door. We were cruising at 120km per hour at the time. I am ashamed to say that along with, "Nooo. Don't!" I also thought. Take the dog with you... It seemed quite incredible to me at the time, that with the world as her oyster, she was blatantly unable to be happy. It is no joke what a miserable childhood can do. And yet she spoke to her father frequently. I suppose he held the purse strings.

He had divorced her mother some years before and that was all Celia would say about her. Toulouse of course, was too provincial but we did stay in a gite halfway between Albi and Gaillac, where I did all the shopping at the local market. I was having fun trying out new foods and recipes. Celia was miserable.

Mitsy was happy. She had an enormous garden to run around in. We stayed five nights. It was a Saturday lunchtime when Celia announced. "I want to go to Paris."

"I know," I agreed. "Lovely city." And I continued to mop up the saffron cream sauce that had surrounded the scallops.

"I mean now. I want to go now."

My strict nanny to naughty child routine had proved useless.

I sighed as I gathered up the plates. At least Celia did eat when I cooked. I realised she was just so damned uncomfortable in public places, it stymied her appetite.

"Do you know how many kilometres it is to Paris?"

I was hoping for a reprieve, at least until the next day when the roads would be quieter. But no, she was already on the phone to daddy in New York. "Where should I stay in Paris?"

I left her to it. I didn't enjoy hearing Celia being shouted at, even though I felt like doing it myself some of the time.

I piled up the dishwasher and dashed next door to the owners of the gite.

Yep, sorry. She wants to leave. No, nothing to do with the gite. She just cannot settle.

I handed over the cash that Celia had withdrawn the day before. Enough to cover the seven nights we were due to stay and a little extra as I wouldn't be able to leave the place spic and span.

Seven hundred kilometers and seven hours later, we arrived in Paris. It was 9 p.m. on a Saturday evening in April and it had begun to sleet. Great.

No need for maps, I know Paris like the back of my hand.

This had been Celia's one rare show of confidence some hours earlier.

Sadly, she meant she knew it by walking and getting taxis, never driving. She had lost her driving licence, not mislaid, she had actually managed to run up twelve points rapidly, back when she was still drinking.

I finally found the right boulevard and was staggered to find ourselves outside a measly 3* hotel in the 14th arrondissment. Such a come down. I knew the George V was not her style but I had hoped, Le Meurice, perhaps. Ah well.

I deposited Celia and Mitsy outside, amidst intermittent car horns. I drove off to find somewhere to park.

My French at that stage was pretty sketchy but I knew parking in Paris was very relaxed compared to the UK. (Things have changed a lot since then) It was still deemed acceptable to park, not just near but actually on zebra crossings! I wouldn't go that far. Plus I was beginning to lose sight of the hotel so I drove round in a loop, in the hope of finding somewhere near the hotel.

I finally parked on a corner. There was a sign. Something about Code #? It was double dutch to me.

Tip # 2. Never assume that because other cars are parked badly, it is okay for you to do the same.

The hotel was small and adequate. I was greeted with raised eyebrows from the concierge. It turned out that Miss Cohen had stayed here before. The raised eyebrows were a look of sympathy towards me.

As usual I had the room next door to Celia. I had insisted, once we had got past the one week trial, that I would not spend more than a few minutes in her room and she was not allowed to smoke in my bedroom. If she wanted to talk for longer she could ring me. Room to room.

My phone rang. "Yes, Celia."

"I want to eat."

It was 10.45p.m. The restuarant downstairs had closed and there was no way I was traipsing around Paris, now that the sleet was beginning to give way to heavy rain.

"There is a Chinese take away opposite. Go and get a menu and bring it to me."

Celia hung up. I had never heard her say please and her thank you's were limited. Like most hotels this one had a, no food in rooms, policy. It was the first time we had stayed somewhere that didn't provide room service. I drew back the net curtain and could read the flashing lights of Peking-Woo.

Getting a menu into the hotel was no problem but Chinese food? You can hardly disguise that aroma...

The concierge conveniently looked the other way when I returned with two large brown paper bags. I guess our Miss platinum-American-Express-card guest, would usually leave a big tip, but I still felt guilty.

I was glad not to go anywhere the next day. I was tired from the long drive. I had slept badly after shovelling too much Chinese food into my system at almost midnight and that damned illuminated sign stayed on all night. The curtains were not thick. I wasn't sure how much more of this I was going to take. I had tried to communicate with Celia. I had phoned the agency only to discover that Christine was on the other line. I bet she was. I had never walked out on a job and Celia could not be left to look after herself.

Money it seemed was no problem. I never seemed to be in that position and watched with envy. But would I have swopped places with Celia? Never.

I was envious that she could speak five languages fluently. But, she flatly refused to use any of them. She insisted that I always order for us in restaurants, even though my French must have made her wince. She was just too shy.

Celia, slept, ate and smoked. She didn't want to go anywhere. She had seen it all in the 60's and 70's. So why were we in Paris, I wondered. I assumed she wanted some familiarity around her but she never went out, except to eat. And oh boy, did we eat. If it had a Michelin star it was okay by Celia. She rarely got past the first course. She would often order a main course, pick at it and say, I'm going back to the hotel. You have what you want. The first couple of time I refused to stay without her and went back to the hotel with her.

Then we went to *Le Benoit*. I knew a few famous French chef's names. Alain Ducasse was one of them. So when Celia started her telltale fidgeting at the end of the amuse bouche, there was no way I was budging. She stayed long enough to be almost amused by my reaction the biggest, whitest asparagus I had ever seen. In between mouthfuls I was trying not to stare at Dustin Hoffman who was hosting a table of ten people. Celia left as I was tucking into the most succulent, pink duck...

She gave me her credit card and nodded at the Maitre'd who seemed to think it perfectly normal for someone else to be signing Celia's credit card slip. (This was pre-pin numbers)

Good job I was honest.

Celia was still taking anti depressants and smoking like a chimney. She was such a sad figure. Her clothes all had designer labels in them but she managed to make them all look drab and shapeless. I left a message with the agency asking them to phone me at the Paris hotel. It was 10 a.m Monday morning and it was snowing. Mitsy had to have her walk but I was to carry her over any puddles. Celia was convinced that Mitsy would get pneumonia and die if she got her undercarriage wet. Carry an umbrella and a dog? That did it. I was back on the phone.

"Please tell Christine I need to speak to her. I will wait if she is on the other line."

"You've done better than anyone else." It was Christine.

"Pardon?"

" I assume you are calling to say you quit?"

"I'm giving Celia and you, one week's...what do you mean I've done better...?"

"Three weeks now?"
"Yep. Miss Cohen is not a new client, is she?"

"I never said she was."

"So, how long?"

"The previous companions?"

" Go on."

"The longest was eight days, the shortest eight hours."

"Wow, I'm up for a long service medal, then."

"Look, can you manage another week? I am going to speak to her father. He controls everything."

"Except his temper." I said without thinking.

" Oh yes. We know. You have done extremely well. What happened to Nice?"

"Long story. I will tell you another time. Just please find someone to take over from me because I'm out of here next Monday."

"Okay, Laura, bon courage. I'll call when we have a solution."

I took Mitsy for her 'walk'. She yapped and snapped at the snow flakes along with all the other three trillion dogs in Paris. I once read there are ten times as many dogs as children in Paris. I believe it. I also believe that piles of dog poo and slippery pavements are not a good combination. I returned a damp (topside only) Mitsy to Celia's smoke filled bedroom and calmly stated that I was giving her one week's notice. Celia said she would like it in writing. To go with all the others, I imagined. I promised to do just that as soon as I had retrieved Celia's other suitcase from the car.

When we had arrived I had taken my suitcase and Celia's from the back seat but left her valuable case in the boot. By valuable I mean, it was filled with her favourite books. Some first editions. Mainly antique art books. The case weighed a ton. We had both forgotten about it yesterday and this morning it was a young girl on reception and I didn't think I could ask for her help. Somewhere in the boot, (Celia called it the trunk) along with the case was a set of strapon wheels. This was going to be fun in this weather. I needn't have worried. I walked to the end of the road, turned the corner and voila, no car!

The cafe on the corner was doing a roaring trade. I knew I was at the right corner. I remembered the name. *Le Bon Coin*. Or not.

"A white Peugeot 106." I asked of the barman.

A customer took great delight in taking me outside and pointing to the sign. Code #...

It was some time later that I discovered, loosely translated, that you can park here until 8 a.m. Monday morning. It was now 10.45 a.m.

Another pastis supping patron explained in broken Ingleesh that the Gendarmes had towed the car away, to the police pound. Wouldn't a parking ticket have done for starters? They don't do things by half in Paris.

I did the only thing possible under the circumstances. I sat down and ordered a coffee.

Someone produced the address for the police car pound. I wondered what the word for smirk was in French. It seemed like a short walk, between metro stops and I thought the sooner I got there the better but Celia was expecting me to return with her suitcase. I wasn't sure how just aware she was of time. She seemed to drift from day to day.

I went straight back to the hotel and smiled at the young woman on reception. She smiled back. I described my plight. She didn't smirk.

Celia, for all her faults, didn't go off the deep end when I explained what had happened. I think she really couldn't be bothered. Phew.

She reached for her credit cards. I explained that to use them she would have to accompany me. This was not going to happen.

The tune, *April in Paris*, somehow seemed totally inappropriate and the fact that it was rattling round in my head, made me laugh. The wind had caught my umbrella and had turned it into a colourful satellite dish. Singing in the rain would have been a better choice. I glanced up to see a Omar sharif look-a-like grinning at me.

"Perdu, madame?"

Yes, I was lost, in almost every sense. I had lost my boss's hire car, possibly her irreplaceable book collection, my job (willingly) and my sense of direction (not much to lose, frankly) but not my sense of humour.

I showed the man with the middle eastern promise, my map. I had been struggling with it when my umbrella gave up its job. The man in the cafe had kindly drawn a red circle around my destination.

Momentarily forgetting I was in Paris, I replied, "Yes."

"Ah, English."

I nodded.

"Don't worry, I know where it is. Not far but with this weather. Come, I will give you a lift."

How sad it is that we have assume everyone is guilty until proven innocent in these situations. I'm sure he was a perfectly respectable man offering help but...

He saw my dilemma.

He took out his wallet and showed me a photo of his wife and three children and his carte d'identitie. He was a Dr. I sighed. The rain was dripping down the back of my neck and my hair was plastered to my head. I shook it, nonetheless.

"Look, I'm sure you are..." I wasn't sure how to continue. He was about ten years older than me, at a guess but I said, "Would you advise your daughter to get into a car with a complete stranger?"

He smiled.

"It is the world we live in...So, let me walk with you."

It was a statement rather than a question.

"Can I ask why you were smiling on such a gloomy day?"

Ah, I thought, here it comes. Would you like to go for coffee, etc, etc?

"I was laughing really, at the absurdity of my situation."

I filled him in with a brief outline of may last three weeks.

"So, you are looking for a job?" His eyes widened like someone hitting the jackpot.

"Well, I would love to stay in Paris but..."

"You must come and meet my wife."

That makes a change, I thought.

" We need a new nanny. We have three children and Vanessa has to go back to the States at the end of the month. She's American." He added, then laughed as he realised his overstatement.

"We would prefer our children to speak English, English. You understand?"

He looked embarrassed.

"Of course. How old are your children?"

I had managed to get my umbrella back to its normal position and close it. Useless piece of...Oops, musn't swear in front of the children. Me, a nanny? I couldn't imagine it.

" Samuel is five. Bettina is three and a half and Jo-Jo is six months. The older two are perfectly tri-lingual and we want to keep this up."

"Amazing."

"Veronique, my wife speaks Arabic to them during the day and I speak French to them in the evenings."

"Wow."

"Adil. I'm sorry, where are my manners. That is my name."

I shook his outstretched hand. We were both soaked and our hands squelched together.

We had been walking at a leisurely pace but now we had reached the Police pound. I pointed with a huge sigh of relief as I saw a low loader deposit the white Peugoet 106 into a parking bay, right by the perimeter wire fence.

"That's it!" I yelped.

Adil gave me a warm smile.

"At least it is safe. Look, here's my card. Phone me at home this evening and we can arrange an interview. Please?"

What can I tell you, my life is bizarre.

A nanny to three children, well one was a baby. What I know about babies you could write on a postage stamp. Food goes in one end and comes out the other.

But I had no other immediate job prospects and despite the awful weather I was in Paris, so I nodded.

Celia could do without me for an hour or two.

I was just going into the main entrance of the police pound when Adil suddenly ran after me.

"Do you think we could say you were in a cafe asking to put up a card for a nanny position and I overheard you?"

This was the second time he had looked embarrassed.

I had to smile.

"I can hardly say, I saw this young woman with beautiful eyes who was smiling despite the rain..."

And he had been doing so well up until that point.

Perhaps there was no wife, children, job etc.

Maybe the photo was a clever ploy.

I could trot along for the interview and never be seen again.

Oh the joys of being a writer and having a stream of 'what if' scenarios at your disposal.

I looked down at the card he had given me.

Dr D**** Adil. Ophthalmologist.

As if reading my thoughts he said. "I always notice eyes."

"Okay," I laughed. "I will call this evening and which cafe did we meet in?"

"Ha! You can have the job. I appreciate someone who takes care of details. Le Bon Coin. Okay?"

" Absoultey. Au revoir and thanks."

So, had he been in the same cafe and followed me. Oh do shut up, Miss Marple and get this car sorted.

I produced my driving licence, my passport (where I do not resemble a drowned rat) and a fistful of French Francs. Celia had emptied her purse adding tersely, that if it was anymore I could pay for it. I was in two minds about this. Yes I had parked the car but she's the one who speaks fluent French. Either of us could have asked at the hotel about the parking restrictions but we didn't. I would consult the agency about this one.

The fee to release the car was 800 Francs. Celia had given me 1000, so that was alright. However there was a parking fine to add to this and points on the driver's licence. Great.

I was allowed to drive the car away on the understanding that I had ten days to pay the fine. I think we'll just gloss over that part.

By the time I got back to the hotel Celia was downstairs in the restaurant...finishing lunch. She waved as I squelched into the foyer.

Alycia (the receptionist) rolled her eyes as I approached.

"Sorry" I dripped onto the polished white tiled floor. At least I avoided the whicker furniture.

Alycia peered over her desk and onto the floor.

"No problem."

I inclined my head towards Celia who was scooping out the last dregs of chocolate ice cream from a very tall glass.

"She's had lunch?" I asked.

"Oh yes. But she has been out."

Alycia said this with such gravity and obviously expected me to know what she was implying.

"But she never goes out..."

Alycia tilted her right hand up to her mouth.

"She's had a drink?"

"She went out in a taxi and came back with a large brown paper bag. We're not responsible for her, of course, but we knew you were out and..."

"Oh, don't worry, what ever you did...?"

"I sent housekeeping into her room. She hates us going in there but..." Alycia sighed. "So sad."

"Alcohol?"

"Oh yes. A large bottle of Vodka. Half empty by the time we got it off her."

"She let you take it?"

"Oui. I mean, yes. She handed it to Margeurite, like a child caught with sweets. So sad."

I was impressed by Alycia's quick response. At least it seemed a hospital visit could be avoided.

"Last time she stayed here she was seeing a , how do you say, a shrink?"

I had to laugh. "Yes, we do say that. Do you remember the name, by any chance?"

Alycia produced a gold embossed card from under the desk.

"He stopped seeing her. She said she was in love with him."

"Oh, okay. I'll give him a try and see if can suggest someone else. Don't suppose she would go to Alcoholics Anonymous."

Alycia frowned at me in such a way that I knew the answer. Not a hope in hell.

I went for the interview that evening with Adil and Veronique. Celia was sleeping off her binge but I made sure there were no cigarettes smouldering before I went out. Alycia promised to look in on her at the end of her shift.

I was back by 9.30p.m.

Adil and Veronique's apartment was to die for. It was a miniature Versaille. Okay, I exaggerate but it resembled a Vogue interiors photo shoot and the fact that they had three children was hard to believe. Not a thing out of place but then there were so many rooms.

They they had just finished their evening meal when I arrived at 8.30p.m. The two older children came up to me and shook my hand. Yep, I could manage a five and three and a half year old. But the moment Veronique lifted the baby from his high chair (Jo-Jo is a boy's name, right?) he started to howl. He had locked eyes with me and wouldn't let go.

I glanced towards Adil who was busy ushering Sammy and Betina off to clean their teeth.

"Have you had a lot of experience with babies?" Veronique seemed to be taking her cue from her youngest.

"Honestly, no I haven't. I'm sorry if I have wasted your time..."

I wasn't sure anything I could say would improve the tension that sizzled between us.

Adil was back and suggesting we all sit down and have a digestive.

Veronique threw him a look that even a blind person would register.

"Thank you but I really must get back to my...erm, the lady I am looking after. She wasn't very well this afternoon."

Great, so now I have just told them that I leave my clients alone when they are sick.

Adil showed me to the door.

He tilted his head on one side. "If you ever have eye problems..."

"I have your card."

I smiled and left.

Men!

Celia's shrink said he could do nothing for her. He gave me another number to try. He told me to lock her anti depressants away for twenty four hours to let the alcohol get out of her system. I spoke to the agency and said she needed more qualified help than we were providing. This was definitely not a hosekeeper/companion job. Celia needed round the clock care.

I had given my notice and Celia hit the bottle. As Alycia rightly said. So sad.

Friday afternoon arrived and I was just about to call London when a Celia clone walked into the hotel lobby.

Only it was a he. One or two people gave him a second glance, he really did look like Woody Allen.

"Miss Cohen's room?" The American drawl and lack of the p word completed my suspicions. Too young to be her father but surely a relative?

"Can I say who is calling?"

It was Alycia back on duty. She had lifted the house phone receiver.

"Room number?" asked Celia-clone.

"I'm sorry sir, I need to speak with Miss Cohen first."

I couldn't let Alycia struggle any longer.

I introduced myself and held out my hand. He took it, shook it and turned back to face Alycia.

"It's okay, I'm just going up. I'll take..."

I waited. Nothing. Blank look from Celia's relative.

"I'm here to see Celia. Where is she?"

"Naturally. And you are?"

Obviously a difficult question for him.

After an exaggerated sigh. "Quentin, Celia's cousin. Didn't the old boy tell you?"

"No. Well, you're here now that's good."

I wondered if the agency knew? Was he taking Celia back to the States?

So many questions but I thought it best to wait.

I knocked on Celia's door, she never locked it, let Quentin in and a considerable amount of smoke, out. About an hour later an envelope slithered under my door. It was handwritten and signed by Celia. It was my final pay, up until the following Monday. It was a cheque in dollars, and a leaflet about weekend events on the left bank. Among them a talk at Shakepseare and Co, one of my all time favourite book shops. She wasn't all bad. In fact I would have loved to known her before she became dependant on drugs of various kinds. She was an absolute mine of information. But the chances of getting the 'real' Celai back were pretty slim, I thought.

Quentin had left a message for me at the desk. Seems this family didn't believe in the personal touch. I was relieved of my duties. Quentin would take care of his cousin from now on. That was it. No details, no thank you. Nothing.

I suddenly felt tired, utterly drained. I sat down in one of the whicker chairs in the lobby. Alycia, bless her, eyed me with concern.

"Cinema!" she announced. "You're free and Paris has cinemas on almost every corner."

She dug out the current copy of *Pariscope*.

"Here!" she pointed to a film showing at the UCG on St Germain. "You will love it and tomorrow, I'm not working, you come out with me."

I was almost in tears. Alycia had to be half my age and she wanted to look after me. I had a carer.

The film I went to see was one of the best I have ever- I won't say seen- best I have ever experienced. Guy Pearce, Terence Stamp and Hugo Weaving in drag.

To this day, the thought and especially the soundtrack from *Priscilla Queen of the Desert* makes me smile. Oh how it lifted my spirits that night. Genius, Alycia.

The next night she took me to the Locomotive night club on boulevard de Clichy. Fabulous. All three floors of it.

We staggered back at 4a.m. My room had been paid for until Monday. I had faxed the agency to stop them sending anyone to replace me.

Alycia's friend's friend, or something like that, offered me a room in her flat for a week, so that I could search for a job. I offered to pay but she said an American student had gone away for a week and the rent was up to date, so no problem. Got to love 'em.

I searched high and low. Literally. The pages of FUSAC, job section. All the local newspapers. W H Smith on rue Rivoli. The Anglican Church notice board. The American church. *Tea and Tattered Pages*, bookshop. Lots of nannying jobs. Live-in, basic wage. No thanks. Hotels. Shops. Nope. Nothing doing.

That April in Paris is one I will never forget. I left one week later, still wondering what became of Celia.

2. Stepford Wives are alive and well on the Riviera.

Or at least they were in 1995.

Lady Blobinger was easy to find. I'm overlooking Regent's park, she explained to me on the phone. We stood in her suspiciously immaculate kitchen. She offered me coffee of the instant variety. Typical. She was sixtyish and stick thin. Short grey hair, white silk blouse with sensible bra underneath, navy pencil skirt and sensible navy shoes. Exciting she was not.

However, I was there for a job interview

Two months in the south of France. Cook/ housekeeper. Own room ensuite.

New villa with a large pool. Twenty minute drive to Cannes. Was there anything she could say that would stop me accepting I wondered.

Lord Blobinger was twenty years older than her and she wanted to spend more time with him.

Lie number one.

So she had decided to hire a little help this summer. I was only five feet, two inches, so I thought I had a good chance.

We mostly eat out.

Lie number two

We have the occasional dinner party for English friends, about twice a month.

Beginning to wish I'd taped this conversation

****

I drove the necessary nine hundred and fifty miles in typical July temperatures.

34° inside the car, only to be greeted by...

" Afraid only got electricity on the ground floor so there is no lighting or hot water in your bedroom or bathroom."

The only thing that had kept me going for the last two hundred miles was the thought of a lovely, lovely bath.

" For supper tonight, I thought we would have something simple."

Lady Blobinger looked pleased with herself.

I was expected to cook after a day's drive? Uh-oh.

A cold shower was quite refresssssinnnggg, but it was still 25° outside. I'd soon recover.

Oh boy, one of my favourite things... A huge, unknown kitchen and just forty five minutes to prepare the first supper. Only the English could want macaroni cheese on a balmy July evening.

I have an allergy to, as in, I throw up, to dairy products. Therefore the prospect of macaroni cheese did not bode well.

Her ladyship's forehead knitted into such contortions when I mentioned my disability that I found myself wondering if the wind blew, her forehead might stick.

I was informed that I may, on this one occasion only, sit at the same table in the dining room with their lord and ladyship. I was placed strategically halfway down the left hand side of the table. Fortunately the salad I had made for myself had ample dressing, so I didn't need the cruet sets, either of them. The table must have been twelve feet long and, pass the salt, please, was a major operation.

Gosh. Better not hold my knife like a dagger.

Whatever happened to...*Of course, one shops in the local market in Grasse twice a week. The most wonderful fresh produce.*

Visions of langoustine, exotic salads, garlic sausage and ever so crusty baguettes had also accompanied me on my journey.

I was still standing in the hallway, car key in hand, when I was told.

"I have breakfast on a tray in my room at 7.30 sharp. Lord Blobinger will have his breakfast in the dining room whenever he gets up."

We then proceeded to have a demonstration of tray laying. The precise measurements of milk and the required temperature, applied to the organic muesli at the very last nano second before serving. To prevent sogginess.

The papaya and kiwi fruit, of which I used to be very fond, were to be removed from the fridge before going to bed and left on the north east facing window sill so as not to get too warm before serving. And I bet you think I'm joking...

I soon discovered Lady Blob and her chums were the British equivalent of Steptford Wives. And they all had at least two homes, one of which was on the French Riviera. They never mingle (shudder) with the locals and only have British friends from the 'right set'.

I had decided to call them the Stepford Wives when I discovered they are programmed to perform and have no imagination.

For example.

1.   They can only cook certain dishes and even then, have to check in their diary to see what they do eat. Fish, chicken, pasta, something with the eggs, lamb cutlets, eat out two nights. Sorted.

2.   When entertaining they buy the most expensive foods, which have to be obvious and mentioned frequently throughout the meal. The rest of the time delicacies such as Campbell's condensed chicken soup are their staple diet.

3.   Eat and drink things they don't really like just to be fashionable

4.   Buy tinned foods and long life cartons but always the same two or three items. Siege mentality?

5.   Have toilet rolls, can't remember what they call them... lavatory paper? Enough to last two months, delivered by John Lewis. They don't like the French ones. I nearly choked to death laughing when the van arrived.

6.   Set the alarm to get up at 11.00 p.m., having being in bed for an hour and half to switch the dishwasher on at a cheap rate. Still wondering whether I should have mentioned...timers! Surely John Lewis could have sent one and a socket adaptor?

7.   Have a silver pill box on the dining table. The lid is never closed. It is too full.

8.   Complete *The Telegraph* crossword while you're still reading the stop press in *The Guardian*.

9. Talk as if they're about to be sick and holding it in their mouths.

10. Place one cocktail stick under the cutlery rack on the draining board to test whether it is moved and therefore cleaned. I couldn't resist adding another one. ;-)

11. At dinner parties just as you're about to start serving, the hostess with mostest asks, "Are we making you nervous?" To which you smile, and say sweetly, "No, not at all." You can save the 'you stupid two faced cow' for when you're back in the kitchen.

12. Treats her husband like a naughty schoolboy even infront of guests.

13. Insist that you switch off one light before putting on another. Get used to walking around in the dark.

14. Has twelve identical bras. All, M and S, or John Lewis, plus thirty odd pairs of pants always worn with panty liners. Presumably because the help does the washing, it cannot be seen that Stepford wives have bodily functions too.

15. Have LUX flakes in the cupboard circa 1976 which has gone rock hard as she never hand washes. Everything goes in the machine. Despite her telling you to the contrary.

16. Honestly believe they are made as something other than flesh and blood. Not like the rest of us.

17. They all compliment each other on their clever, original flair for interior design.

Had to resist temptation to paste exact replica of Lady Blob's drawing room, from last month's *Country Homes* magazine, up on the wall.

18. They call each other by their titles, as if they'd lose them otherwise.

19. Go swimming in their pool, in the nude. Ask that you avert your eyes when they do so. Erm, yes please!

20. Keep a book of all their dinner parties. Not just a guest list but little sketches of where everyone was sat. (All were seated, my mistake.)

21. Have to go shopping everyday but never quite get everything. This can be simply achieved. Example: A six bedroom house, only buy four bedside lamps and bingo must go shopping again tomorrow. In the case of Lady Blob (a term of endearment on my part). I can't help but notice, not only did she go shopping every morning but she always came back with very little but in a much better mood. Her husband was, she correctly told me the interview, a good 20 years older than her. I'm saying nothing.

22 Gasps in real horror when she catches you drinking Coca-Cola. "Oh how could you? All that sugar. It's so bad for you." You can see her watching you, expecting you to curl up and die like putting salt on a slug.

22. Have to be told that her husband of thirty odd years, the man at the other end of the table, the one with his own cruet, doesn't actually like nutty bread . He's only got three of his own teeth left. He dislikes funny shaped pasta. What's wrong with spaghetti he asks. Not in company, darling, tomato sauce, chin, that sort of thing.

23. Always phone each other the morning after a dinner party to say just how delightful it was, darling. You must come back to us soon.

24. Bring out the same crisps that didn't get eaten at the last two forays. Champagne and stale crisps. Super.

25. Have a little bell to ring for the end of each course. This is fine except when the average age of the diners is ninety three. It is hard to tell whether they finished eating or just don't have the energy to go on.

26. Insist you serve from the left, naturally, even if it means moving guest's walking frames, portable oxygen, nebulizers etc, out of reach.

27. Expect an expensive gift which will be barely unwrapped before being relegated to the bottom of the drinks trolley. The Hermes or Cartier wrapping being of more significance than the gift itself.

28. Offer guests coffee at the end of the meal. All decline except the ninety five year old Countess, who, either hasn't heard or just likes the idea of any kind of a stimulant!

29. Never say please but will occasionally say kue as in, than-kue.

30. On rare occasions will ask if you enjoyed your afternoon off but walk away before giving you chance to reply.

31. Has two other homes each with its own clapped out automatic Honda, Nissan or Volvo.

32. Have to lie down in the middle of the morning dreadfully upset when the automatic pool cover won't work. And the electrician can't come until after lunch.

33. Have to delay doing T*he Telegraph* crossword by twenty minutes to have a little weep and find her calculator when she receives the news that her father has died.

34. I think you get the picture...

*****

The only job I ever left before completing my contract. I never did get a contract. And her word turned out to be as reliable as a chocolate teapot. Each Friday evening I tried to broach the subject of my job description/conditions and pay. Her answer was always the same. *I don't have time to discuss it now*. There was no agency to back me up so after six weeks out of the eight I packed and left.

I was paid on a Friday evening, the paltry sum of a thousand French francs (approximately £100) This being in relation to catering for a dinner party for six people, maximum once every two weeks. In reality it was eight people three times a week. The cleaner was on holiday or had left. Who knows...?

I left a note for her explaining my reasons for leaving. And I left one for him apologising for the fact that the control freak at the other end of the dining table was about to become even more insufferable.

He had my condolences.

As I drove away and the barrier to the gated exclusive community lifted I felt a pang. I had been mean. They had guests arriving in less than forty eight hours and I had overheard her on the phone giving them all the wrong access code. A trivial point and of course two wrongs don't make a right.

The straw that broke my back? Cleaning her bathroom (1 of 4 in the house) and she offers me an old toothbrush. It's good for cleaning between the tiles. She says in all seriousness. Having momentarily visualised where I thought the toothbrush would look best...that's when I had decided to pack.

****

Here are some outtakes. Thanks to speech recognition.

The correct version is on the second line.

- 20 minute strike in Tunis

20 minute drive to Cannes.

- Visions of it because attic salads

Visions of langoustine and exotic salads.

- Standing in the hallway and khaki in hand

Standing in the hallway, car key in hand.

- British equivalent to deptford wives.

British equivilent to Stepford wives.

- A trivial point and of course two wrongs don't make a writer.

Two wrongs don't make a write. Ha, ha, right.

- deep pool cover won't work annually to let Russian COD come until after lunch.

Dreadfully upset when the automatic pool cover won't work and the electrician can't come until after lunch.

- the EU should you be toothpaste

the 'you stupid two faced cow'

- Bring out the Saint Christopher

Bring out the same crisps.

- Expect an expensive deficit

Expect an expensive gift.

- The her maize or Cartier wrapping

The Hermes or Cartier wrapping

- A slow death coffee of to the mill

Offer guests a coffee after the meal.

So you see, there is room for improvement with speech recognition but every cloud… ;-)

3. Miss Babs.

Elegant was not sufficient a word. Barbra, spelled the same as the iconic singer, was a picture from the cover of *Harpers and Queen,* circa 1976. The fact that she was 79 and this was 2006 seemed to have passed her by.

Barbra was not at all happy that the agency had divulged her age; after all I was there to look after her husband. She just needed help, occasionally.

Tip # 3 People either totally under or over- estimate their need for help. So arrive with an open mind.

Miss Babs (as I was soon to call her behind her back) led me into the spacious drawing room. Each wall sported a gilt framed mirror. This way, Miss Babs could see herself at any given moment.

"Bunny dahling, this lovely young lady has to come to help us. Do say hello."

It took a while but I fathomed the term of endearment came from William- Billy- Bunter to Bunny.

Bunny was a great bear of a man, hunched in his armchair with a cut glass tumbler of whiskey in one hand and about half an inch of smouldering cigar in the other.

"Really Bunny, dahling, it IS only eleven thirty. A little early don't you think?"

This was the start of many pointless conversations that I would hear over the next ten days. No, not two weeks, I was trying to get out of doing couples but the agency pleaded and so here I was. I say conversations but that implies a two way street. Bunny's replies were always the same.

"It's only a little one. First one today in fact, old girl..."

At this point he would wave the extremely heavy looking tumbler, about in the air.

This would prompt Barbra to rush forward and retrieve the offending article.

"Have you any idea how much it costs to have these Persian rugs cleaned these days?"

She suddenly turned her attention to me.

"You do know, they must not be vacuumed, don't you?"

"Of course!" I lied.

This is how you learn most of the dos and dont's, especially in some of the rather well –to-do, households.

The lady of the house I soon discovered was the mistress of overstatement. My stay was punctuated by great events such as these…

Ten minutes into my break, I heard.

"Where are you? There's a flood in the kitchen."

I ran downstairs.

"Oh dear. Where?"

She points to the sink.

"There are a few spots of water on the draining board."

I burst out laughing.

I refrained from saying 'Shall I call a plumber?'

***

Bab's cuppa was due at 7.40 a.m.

The next morning I must have spent a fraction too long in the bathroom before making the early morning drinks as I was greeted with.

"You're three minutes late this morning."

Amazing how the offending cup didn't tip up.

***

I said. One and *a half* inches of orange juice.

***

Day 1. Empty the dishwasher before we come down.

Day 2. Don't leave Bunny on his own....to empty the dishwasher.

***

It was a game. Let's see. Whatever I do it will be wrong...

There was no fresh meat or fish and only two vegetables (beans and broccoli) over nine days.

I swear I could feel a bout of scurvy coming on.

Every meal was pre-prepared, convenience stodge.

On the last but one day (I almost made it) I went out and bought a salad.

***

Barbra seems to want to make life difficult, especially for her husband. It doesn't take much to realise that she feels deeply betrayed by this sham of a husband that he had become due to his alcohol related dementia.

I say. Okay Bunny stand up now...and he does.

She says. Bunnykins just put your left hand on the table and move that cushion and get hold of her elbow and now stand up...and nothing.

So this gives her an opportunity to shout at him.

***

I once dared to glance at the newspaper headlines as I walked past the kitchen table.

She rushed over and folded the newspaper so that only bottom of the back page was showing.

***

And even worse, I was putting rubbish out as the district nurse pulled into the drive so I let her in through the back door.

Quelle horreur. Poor Babs couldn't get her breath for a moment...

"You let the district nurse in through the garage?"

I couldn't imagine why this could cause such consternation...

***

Their granddaughter was apparently in New Zealand.

There was a postcard from Wellington on the fridge door.

I glance at and comment. "Been there. Lovely, it was."

Barbra snatches it away, putting it into her cardigan pocket.

***

Miss Babs suddenly feigns interest in my family.

"So what does your father do?"

Ooh the temptation to lie. Extremes seemed the most tempting.

'He's in prison for impersonating a transgender version of the Queen' or 'He's cultural attaché to the British ambassador in the Bahamas."

"He's an accountant."

That allowed Miss Babs to look suitably unimpressed.

"Of course most of my family have careers in the medical profession."

"I've had 30 operations, you know."

She said this as if it was something to be proud of?

Perhaps with the family connections it was, have one operation, get a second one free?

"Our eldest granddaughter is having to work in a Birmingham hospital at the moment."

I waited. There was obviously more.

"Where is Dudley, exactly?"

"In the West Midlands. How's she getting on?"

"It's full of dreadful Birmingham people!"

She got me on that one. I couldn't think of a suitable repost.

***

4   Don't open any windows. All the frames are rotten.

I suppose I should have expected it. Damp. Everywhere. Is it to do with being surrounded by water? I was on a small island off the coast of northern France but it was English to a tee.

The first time I had flown, as a young teenager, it had been to Jersey. It had seemed very exotic back then.

Today, just two days until Christmas and I have arrived in what can only be described as a residence of former elegance, now in a state of total disrepair.

The niece, I say *the* niece, as she was the only surviving member of this mysterious family, was there to greet me. I was not given the name until I arrived. Let's just say a small empire was known with this name. And she will inherit this pile one day, if she can bear to live here.

Tip #4. Use Google earth (didn't exist when I was doing this) to check out just how remote the place is.

The house was cavernous, with the most ridiculously large hall I had ever seen.

A twelve foot Christmas tree stood at the bottom of the grand sweeping staircase. There were forty seven steps, a semi landing and the kind of curve that must have sent the stairlift, (yes, all the way to the top) salesperson into a spasm of excitement. Bet that was an order worth having.

The polished wooden floor of the hall meant that it was impossible to move about quietly. This continued into the breakfast room and kitchen. The kitchen alone was the size of a three bed semi in suburbia.

Sure enough there was the Robert's radio complete with leather handle and plastic dial, in cream. There were five doors leading from the kitchen. One to the larder, (which reeked of damp) the wine cellar (cobweb city) the electric meters (recognisable from old episodes of Upstairs, Downstairs) a passageway that led to the coal scuttle and the fifth door was locked and even the niece didn't know what was behind it.

"Well, I'll be off then. Have a lovely Christmas" The niece was donning a Barbour, green wellies and a flowerpot- man hat, in green naturally.

Hey, not so fast, I thought. I haven't even been introduced to my charge, or shown my room...

I opened my mouth but before I could speak, the niece extracted a fat envelope. Cash. I had signed up for three weeks, god help me, and now she was paying me in advance? This had never happened before. Ever.

"You will stay, won't you?"

The look in her eyes registered somewhere between terror and exhaustion.

"I will be back before the new year. Whenever I can get a flight."

Pleading now.

"And you can phone every day. Anytime. Really. Oh and don't try to open any of the windows, all the frames are rotten!"

With that she was gone, scurrying out of the back door like a Jack Russell after a rabbit.

A strange tinkling noise somewhere around the hall, from which I had just come, sent me back to see what was happening.

I thought maybe a bauble had fallen off the tree.

"So, has she paid you? Cash, right?"

The tinkling sound turned out to be about three dozen bangles competing for space on the left arm of a woman I had never seen before.

Wrapped from head to toe in a multi-coloured, striped, woollen poncho, for want of a better word, was Gladys, I would soon find out.

I nodded at her question.

"Last Christmas, she left, the carer, I mean on Boxing Day. Got a boat to France. Funny that 'cause there weren't no boats going nowhere that day. Anyway, you met the old girl yet?"

I shook my head, still mesmerised by this newcomer who seemed intent on bringing as much colour to this damp, grey, dismal day as possible. Even her hair was multi coloured. A bright burgundy red with orange streaks.

"Bit o' henna, bit o' tint. Like it?"

I had obviously been staring at her head.

"Yeah, great. So you're...?"

"Dear god didn't she didn't she tell yer nothing?"

"Not a lot, no. She seemed in a hurry to leave."

At this, Gladys threw back her head and laughed with enough force to shake the decorations...

"Are you there?" shrieked a voice from upstairs.

Gladys gave me an inane smile.

I thought about the money. I thought about shoving it straight in her hand and making a run for it, straight out of the front door.

"You'll be fine, just try not to let 'er get to you. You get three hours off instead of two by the way, you'll need it."

I wondered if I started to cry, would they deem me unsuitable for the job?

"Come on, the cat needs to see the mouse."

With that Gladys took me by the elbow and guided me up the winding staircase.

"Guy who put this in," says Gladys, tapping the stair lift as we passed at the top. "Bought his self a fuckin' yacht."

I nodded a smile.

"First door on the left. Go on in and introduce yerself. She won't remember yer name but it's the only thing to do."

"All I will say is this; don't camp out on the landing. One carer brought a kettle, table and chair up here. "

Gladys saw my expression. "To save keep coming up and downstairs every time she calls yer."

"Oh, ok." Was all I could manage.

I had known about the two cats but as I said, I had no idea of the lady. This was very unusual but then the whole place was like something out of a potential horror movie. The two Siamese cats both had black, gem studded, collars. Madam had a sequined, turquoise bed jacket over white silk pyjamas.

Gladys, seeing my look of trepidation, followed me into the bedroom.

"You still not dressed, yer lazy devil."

"See, see," Madam is looking at me. "This is what I have to put up with. Who are you? I don't know you. What are you staring at?"

"I do apologise erm..."

"Just call 'er anything you fancy. Her name's Elinor but she never remembers, do yer darlin'."

"Pleased to meet you, Elinor. And what are the cat's names?"

Elinor creases up her eyes and they disappear into the folds of very tired skin.

"Where is Meredith? I demand to see her. At once."

The niece? I mouth at Gladys. She nods.

The one name she can remember.

And as if to prove the point, Elinor leans back against her pillow and hollers.

"Mer- a- dith!"

"You'll hear a lot of that."

Gladys takes hold of my arm and guides me back onto the landing.

"Keep stalling for as long as you can 'cause once she knows Meredith has left the building," at this, Gladys rolls her eyes. "All hell will be let loose. Trust me."

"I do," I faltered. Like I had a choice!

"Just say stuff like, Meredith's on the phone or gone to the shops. You'll work it out. Like I say, stall her. It's the only way."

We had reached the half landing. There was an enormous window, looking out towards the bay. Sadly, the glass was so tarnished with green mould etched in the corners, it was impossible to see out. Gladys followed my gaze and shrugged.

"Oh and don't worry if either of the cats peg out. Dear old Elinor tends to feed them her pills. You have to stay in the room while she takes 'em. Three in the morning, three at night. She'll put 'em in her mouth, stick her tongue out to show you but there's no guarantee she'll swallow 'em. Do what you can. Me number's written in the kitchen, your sitting room, your bedroom. You seen it yet?"

"No, do I want to?"

Gladys let rip with one of her raucous laughs which sadly seemed to set Elinor off, again.

"Are you there? MER_A_DITH!"

"You will have to ignore twice and placate the third time, that's what the others have done. Any questions?"

So many…

"Come on downstairs. Let's have a cuppa, and then I can show you yer room."

"You think tea will be strong enough? I mean we are not allowed to drink on duty but honestly…"

Gladys did something I imagine she had done many times before. She draped her jangly arm around my shoulders and gave me a hug. Her eyes said. You can do it. My head agreed but my heart was sinking by the minute.

"Look here's the intercom but you 'ardly need it. There's nowt wrong with 'er lungs."

The sound of the solid oak front door closing behind Gladys, felt like the beginning of a prison sentence. Then I remembered my 'life is what you make it' lecture that I recited mentally to myself at these moments.

It went like this. Take down the Calendar. Mark the days. Count the days. Write in the bottom right hand corner the amount earned. The equivalent of putting coins in a sweetie jar. Watch it mount up. From experience I had found that day three and especially night three was the worst. It would seem as if time was being cruelly stretched out with the sole purpose of making you question your mode de vie. After three days your worst fears have been realised. The client is mad, one of the cats is incontinent and nothing in the pantry has a sell by date that can guarantee a botulism free stay.

Doing this job is a bit like that old television series...*And who lives in a house like this*?, except you already know. Still, it is fascinating to be able to rummage through people's pantries, guilt free, in the hope of finding some rare and edible delicacy. Large square biscuit tins are always a source of delight...well usually.

Ooh, mince pies. Things were looking up. I poured myself another cup of tea and placed a mince pie, they looked homemade, on to a plate when the sound of Elinor's voice came reverberating over the baby monitor.

"Are you there?"

Count...1.

I bit into the mince pie. Ouch. It was as hard as a rock. The last thing I needed was a broken tooth at Christmas. Just then the phone rang.

"It's me." It was Gladys.

"Forgot to say the housekeeping purse is in the bread bin. Two hundred quid. Go out tomorrow and get what you need. The last one didn't do no proper shoppin'. Reckon you'll need to stock up. Won't be no deliveries from the mainland to shops 'ere 'til after Christmas or even New Year, if weather's bad."

"Oh, right, thanks, I'll go in my time off."

"Yep, yer can't leave the dragon unattended."

Despite Gladys's description I had the distinct feeling that she was actually very fond of Elinor. It turned out that Gladys had been Elinor's companion after Elinor's husband had died but since the demons, as Gladys called Elinor's dementia had set in, it all became too much, hence full time carers were installed.

I had assured Gladys that I would wait for the, aptly named, relief carer to arrive before setting off on my adventure to the shops the next morning.

I prayed it would stop raining by then and that the car, aka, a sewing machine on wheels would manage to negotiate any steep hills between here and the shops.

"Are you there?"

Count... 2

I binned the mince pie and started to search for something sweet and edible. The bread bin, as promised contained a small brown, snap top purse but no bread. I checked the fridge. Nope. I finally found two slices of Hovis wrapped in cling film in the freezer. The cling film of course had long since parted company with the bread, leaving the slices a whiter shade of brown. Toast was the only solution.

Tip #4. Always check the setting on the toaster as some over enthusiastic cleaner will have knocked the dial up to 5 whilst wiping down the ancient, grey and red spotted Formica work surface.

Elinor''s high pitched scream, "Mer-a-dith!" was just audible over the sound of the smoke detector as it shrieked.

'Toast is...cremated.'

A lot of old houses have high ceilings. Smoke detectors are invariably placed high enough to be completely out of reach to anyone less than six feet, four inches tall. At five feet two, the only option is a stool and a tea-towel.

I did a precarious helicopter impersonation as Elinor continued to try and out do the smoke detector in both volume and pitch.

I finally found at the bottom of a pile of biscuit tins, some so rusty, you couldn't get the lids off, an old Tupperware container. It was like finding gold. An unopened packet of Bourbon biscuits. Expiry date? Impossible to read. I tore it open and tipped the contents onto a Wedgewood plate.

They looked a tad pale for bourbons and the Channel Islands are not covered by the NHS so I was taking a risk. Which will kill me sooner, the pale bourbon imitations or my inability to cope with, Elinor, who suffers from *slight* dementia. Another agency understatement…

What a Christmas this was going to be.

The relief carer duly arrived the next morning. She was a regular. She admitted that three hours was more than enough and couldn't understand how we did our job.

Of course it was still raining and the lane down to the house was full of potholes. I didn't recognize the make of the car but it seemed to be about as sturdy and reliable as those old Trabants. I found what was laughingly called the village. It consisted of two almost identical shops. Imagine the average corner shop on two levels. There were two of them both selling the same things.

Maybe I was just unfortunate to find a corner of this apparently wealthy idyll but it seemed to be residing in the equivalent of a barely postwar Northern Britain.

I parked behind the two level corner shop and huddled with everyone else in the glass lift that went up to the next floor

No one smiled. No one spoke. Great. At least now I could buy some decent food. I clutched the small brown purse as if it were some life- saving appliance.

The first thing I noticed was the magazine rack. It was almost empty. The newspaper section was also similarly deplete. Plenty of copies of the local paper and the *Racing Post*, with very little else.

I remembered what Gladys had said about shops not being stocked until after Christmas. I didn't even want to imagine that the weather would stay like this until after the New Year. I didn't want to buy lots of magazines and newspapers but I did at least want to have a choice.

I soon discovered the fresh food section was about as useless as the newsagents department. There was an exceptionally poor selection of cheeses. To think that we were nearer to the French mainland than the UK. What a travesty. Cheddar, Stilton and a very dried up looking Brie. The salad section typically had iceberg lettuce. That crunchy, completely tasteless stuff. The woman just ahead of me took the last bag of spinach.

With two days to go, the food shopping frenzy that ensues just before Christmas had certainly taken hold here. I was beginning to fantasise about boats to France on Boxing Day.

I eventually gave up and started to load the trolley with frozen and tinned goods.

A gourmet Christmas was not going to happen.

Small plastic buckets and spades in every colour, still dangled by the checkout tills. They were covered in dust. Still no one smiled. It was like a very bad London suburb.

At least on Guernsey people were friendly. ..

Just writing this now is making me feel depressed. So imagine what it was like in reality!

I made the most of my three hours off by driving around looking for a café. At least a coffee would help, possibly. Surely decent coffee existed here? I wasn't worried about the frozen food thawing. The heater in the car didn't work. I didn't go too far as I was struggling to remember how to get back along many an unnamed lane with a distinct lack of signposts. Had anyone tell them the war was over and it was OK to have signposts up now?

Anyone reading this from the Jersey tourist board will not be my friend. But I'm just telling it like it was circa 2005 in St Lawrence. That was the area of this god forsaken island I had been deposited in. It must have some nice parts surely. Can it only be a tax haven, I wondered.

I returned to my prison, two hours and fifty minutes later, sans coffee. I decided I wouldn't relax until I got back and didn't want to take the risk of 'wasting' time in a café.

The first smile I had seen all day was on the relief carer's face. She told me she was from Madeira. She spoke English and Portuguese. She was living with her boyfriend and two small children in a very damp loft converted into a flat, over a garage. She wasn't kidding.

She invited me round for cup of tea a few days later when another carer was in situ.

As I climbed the stairs to the right hand side of the garage the smell of damp hit me. It took my breath away.

It really is the most disgusting smell. When she said small children, she actually meant one was a baby. The baby's cot was up against the wall that was covered in black spores.

She was desperate to leave. She wanted to know about work in England. I had no idea how easy that would be for her but I promised to make enquiries. The owners of the property were away until after the New Year but this young couple and their children were not allowed to use of any part of the house. I couldn't imagine that it could be any worse.

Who was I kidding? My bedroom had been a revelation. The first thing on my shopping list the morning after I arrived was air freshener and some scented candles. What it really needed was a dehumidifier and a damp proof course. I had told myself I would get used to the smell. After a while I took to sleeping on the sofa in one of the downstairs rooms. It was the only one that had been decorated and had a new carpet in the last fifty years. There was a modern plasma television. They had become all the rage and plenty of channels to choose from. Lots of videos and dvds. So all was not lost. The door was to be kept closed so the cats couldn't ruin the carpet and the furniture which they had done just about everywhere else. Thank goodness the cats used the litter trays that were provided in her bedroom, on the landing, in the hall and in the kitchen.

My best friend phoned as he always does on Christmas morning and he immediately said. "That bad eh?"

"Oh yes." I replied.

Christmas meant nothing to Elinor. It was just another day. That suited me fine. I like to go the whole hog or not all. Never really been one for half measures.

Elinor had a television in her room and she seemed soothed by the Christmas carols being played on whatever tv channel she had found.

Meredith explained she wouldn't phone. She would leave that to me. Speaking to Elinor on the phone was always a bad idea. It only served to remind her that Meredith wasn't there.

Some days Elinor got dressed and sometimes it was just too much of a battle. She would ask me what was the point? And I seriously struggled to answer her. She had no phone calls and no visitors. The only signs of life were supplied by the relief carers and Gladys, god bless her.

The niece arrived the day I left. She couldn't get a flight any sooner, she apologized.

Gladys had told me that the niece was merely marking time, waiting for her aunt to expire. The niece was already wealthy having been left a large sum by her parents but she seemed intent on what she saw as her rightful inheritance, even though she clearly loathed the place…

But to claim the right to the property she had to be in residence for so many days of the year and she couldn't sell it to anyone else.

I doubted the property could be restored without it costing more than a complete rebuild.

I tried to imagine what it might have been like in its heyday. I struggled. Best to have it razed to the ground and a new modern, damp free, metal window frame- free, green glass panes- free, structure with a view across the bay. I guess that was what she was aiming at.

In the meantime Elinor could not be moved from her home; although it was debatable she knew where she was. A small fortune was being paid out daily not just for her care but trying to heat the damp house with an oil fired boiler that rattled and burped twenty four hours a day.

Gladys new only too well, Elinor would have been much better off in a nursing home but this would contravene the rules relating to the niece inheriting the property so there she stayed.

I could tell you how excruciatingly frustrating it was to be shouted at all day and some of the night but at least I got to walk away after three weeks with a very clear lesson that money so often does not buy you happiness.

And as two the young couple with the children… the next time I went round to the flat above the garage they had gone. Where to? I have no idea. This was before we all had mobile phones as a matter of course and so I had no contact numbers for them.

The carer coming to take over from me on the 3rd of January had been before. I didn't wait around to ask how on earth she managed to do it. I was off the airport in a taxi. My flight wasn't due for four hours but it was the only flight of the day and I just wanted to be in the wonderfully named, departure lounge, where surely they had decent coffee.

I had never found a nearby café to where I was working. I did venture into the capital, St Helier, one day. What a disappointment that was. Okay it was midway between Christmas and New Year but I couldn't help but compare it to some kind of ante room between heaven and hell. It was devoid of any atmosphere.

I could only suppose the tax haven-ists must go somewhere warm and dry during this period.

When the embarkation sign came up for the flight to Gatwick I would have offered to fly the plane myself, if necessary.

5. Hat, scarf, gloves, goodnight.

If I had not known I was in Wales I would have thought I was in Ireland.

For the man standing before me could easily pass as a leprechaun, any day. I knew I was in Wales and it was summer. A good way to remember this, according to one (full sized neighbour) was that the rain was warmer in summer.

That may be true but the rain was just as wet, especially when I realised the only way I could get a signal, aka contact with the outside world on my mobile was to walk across a field of sheep to a hillock. This of course rhymes with how I felt, standing there in a force eight gale, umbrella inside out, waving my phone about desperately trying to get those magic words, connected to O2, to appear on the screen.

Tip # 5. A little isolated= in the middle of frigging nowhere.

This was the first time I had looked after a client who was registered blind and my short term memory powers were about to be severely tested. What drives most clients mad is the disruption to their homes (in an unintentional way) by carers who can't remember where they found a particular jug, map, book, carving knife etc, etc. Things just don't get put back in the same place. The extreme of this, is when well meaning (aka bossy) carers go into a client's home where they have been living, probably for the best part of fifty years and decides to rearrange things, a little. If the carer has sole charge of the kitchen then it's not so bad but if you are still sharing that domain with the lady of the house, you will have your work cut out.

You would think, for example that salt might be located by the hob and coffee near the kettle. In most cases it is but why oh why were kitchen rolls stored in an airing cupboard and marmalade locked in a filing cabinet in one house?

So, back to my leprechaun. He stood just five feet tall and probably weighed about eight stone. He had long bony fingers, a mass of dark curly hair and a thin pointy nose. He was wearing so many layers of clothing I may have misjudged his weight. It was August but that didn't stop him from wearing his favourite cream coloured Arran jumper, dark green trousers and a red bobble hat and you see why I renamed him...Shaun.

Shaun greeted me with, "Ah, a lovely smile!"

I turned to his outgoing carer. She just smiled.

"Didn't you know you can hear a smile?!" Shaun gently mocked me.

"Oh yes, that's true."

I took his outstretched right hand and shook it gently.

"She'll do," he laughed. "Do your worst, Greta and be thorough."

It usually takes about an hour to an hour and a half to go through the house and its occupants' quirks and foibles. I could imagine this would be longer. I'd had a four hour train journey so was in desperate need of a cup of tea. It always amazes me just how 'uncaring' outgoing carers seem to be. I guess they are just frantic to do the handover and leave.

In one case, she did just that. No handover, just pointed to a notebook on the kitchen table and said. It's all there. And with that she slammed the door and was gone.

Greta was the exact opposite. She had been coming here for the last two years, on and off. There is a great advantage to taking over from someone who knows the client so well but also the downside is that they will give you so much information that you cannot possibly take it all in.

I find myself saying. Okay well I'm sure you've got it all written down. But that never stops them. They want to make sure all the i's are dotted and the t's crossed.

It was two hours later when I waved Greta goodbye and promised her that I would phone if I had any queries, whatsoever.

Shaun was standing behind me in the hall as I closed the door behind me.

"She means well but she does go on, doesn't she."

I nodded. Shaun chuckled and I felt foolish as I realised he couldn't see my body language but I was soon to find out, he could sense it.

  Shaun winked at me. Which somehow seemed strange and I don't know why it should, his eyelids still worked perfectly.

"You go and unpack. She showed your room I presume?"

"Oh yes," I replied. "The one with a lovely outlook of across the hills."

It suddenly struck me just how important my surroundings were to me. How long had Shaun been registered blind? I couldn't remember. He was aware of light and dark and movement I had been told, but no real detail. I couldn't imagine relying on memories.

It was at that moment I realised that Shaun had an acute ability to sense what you were thinking. He didn't need to read expressions. Even silence didn't stop him from interpreting a situation correctly.

"And it would be even better if it stopped raining, wouldn't it?"

Shaun chuckled as he waved his hands at me shooing me in the direction of the stairs.

"I'm sure we'll be just fine. Now I am going to sit in my recliner and recline."

It was already 3.30 and Shaun normally had a cup of tea at 4.30 but today he said all rules were temporarily suspended. He would have his cup of tea and cake at 5.00.

My bedroom was located at the back of the house with no street lights to keep me awake and no traffic to do the same.

Only fields and sheep. It should have been a calming viewpoint but I suddenly felt totally trapped. Not an unusual feeling in the first few hours of an assignment. Some places are a lot easier to adapt to than others.

I had been met at the railway station. It had all been arranged.

I had explained to Greta the week before that I was five feet, two inches and blonde. And if by chance there was an influx of other similar travellers arriving at this miniscule backwater on the Welsh border, I added. I will be bringing a red case and a black case.

Impossible to miss I thought.

My train arrived on time. I was the only person fitting my description and once all the other travellers had dispersed there was just one man left standing, leaning against his car. I went up to the man and asked are you waiting for Laura?

He looked me up and down. "That I am."

"Well here I am."

"But," he replied. "I was told you would be wearing a red and black cape."

I had to laugh. "Were you expecting wonder-woman?"

He shook his head, looking thoroughly puzzled.

I wasn't sure how long the drive would be from the station to the house but I had a feeling it was going to go extremely slowly.

It did.

Over the years I had occasionally wondered what it would be like to lose your sight. I would wander round the house with my eyes closed. I could imagine the practical things. Place one finger inside a glass as you pour a cold drink to know when to stop. That kind of thing but it was impossible really to grasp the idea as your mind was fully aware that you could open your eyes at any moment and normal service would be resumed.

The daytime was easy. Shaun liked a chat, or sometimes left undisturbed, to listen to the radio and his meals on time. He sat on a stool up to the breakfast bar in the kitchen as he explained. Less distance from the plate to his mouth. He asked what we would be having to eat for his midday meal whilst he was eating his breakfast.

When I suggested Roast chicken with all the trimmings and an apple and blackberry crumble, his eyes nearly popped out of his head.

"You would do all this?"

"Yes. I love cooking."

"How long you here for?"

"Two weeks." I smiled.

"Real roast potatoes?" He asked.

"Oh yes, nothing but."

We were off to a good start. It actually makes me miserable when people don't care about food.

Shaun needed to have his food arranged on his plate in a certain order. For some reason I wasn't so good at remembering this. For example. Meat at six o clock. Not too much gravy. Mashed potatoes at twelve o- clock and other vegetables in between. I could understand he wanted some idea what he was putting in his mouth before he tasted it.

"I can smell it."

He exclaimed. He was walking in the hall at the time.

"It smells great."

Not everyone enjoys cooking but for me half the pleasure is in the preparation and the ensuing aromas. Agas are brilliant for this. Somehow fragrant cooking smells permeate the house far more easily than from a conventional oven.

For such a tiny man, Shaun had an amazing appetite. He said he quite understood if I wanted to eat somewhere else. He was afraid his table manners lacked finesse since he had lost his sight. He really wasn't that bad. The occasional blob of gravy on the chin but nothing drastic. It was also his way of saying; please don't watch me so I sat at the kitchen table at a ninety degree angle to him, rather than directly opposite.

Bedtime, I soon discovered was a whole other story. A ritual that took the best part of an hour. Shaun could manage his dentures (thank goodness) I don't mind cleaning them I just hate it when people suddenly plonk them in your hand. Slimey…

The confident man that was daytime Shaun became extremely anxious Shaun of the night time. I imagined most of his world must almost disappear once the daylight had gone. So it made sense. He insisted that everything was in its place he would do his best not to disturb me during the night. There was the monitor in the carer's room as usual with the other half in the client's room.

I always had to turn it down to as low as it would go. My hearing is pretty acute even when I'm asleep. Shaun finally climbed into bed wearing just as many clothes as he had during the day. Except for the scarf he didn't tend to wear a scarf during the day. The adult equivalent of a comfort blanket I guess.

The final check was under the pillow. Two handkerchiefs, two mints, two boiled sweets, and what was to become the bane of my life, the talking watch.

An extremely useful thing that even the partially sighted would find beneficial but not so good for those with very good hearing.

The first night passed without a word from Sean as promised.

I went in at 7.30 with a cup of tea. He was sitting bolt upright, smiling. I knew what the next question would be and I just had to lie. Did you have a good night? Was the bed comfortable?

I had a terrible night hardly any sleep but nothing to do with the bed. How Shaun managed to be so bright and breezy considering we had the same amount of sleep, was beyond me. It is only just occurred to me that may be he managed to check his watch while he was still asleep.

I guess that was possible. He could do it out of habit and not even really hear it. His hearing wasn't perfect. So maybe again it was a comfort thing.

But I heard it all right.

Click. The Time is now 1.15 AM. It was said very slowly and clearly. As was, the time is now 3.05 AM. And then 4.45 AM.

By the time the clockwork voice told me it was 7.05 AM I was ready to take a hammer to it.

I couldn't tell Shaun. He obviously, totally relied on it.

But after two very disturbed nights I turned off the monitor. Small though he may be, his voice was good and strong and if he called me during the night I was sure to hear him.

The next day it was wet and windy and yes I was still in Wales. I managed to find the one and only spot with a reception for my mobile phone. Who knew I could be persuaded to walk through a field of sheep, to find text messages as proof that life went on without me. The following day the weather was just too awful, so I decided to walk to the other end of the village where there was a pub. With a bit of luck this one sold coffee as I'm not much of a drinker.

The tiny weather beaten sign swinging in the wind declared Prince of Wales. Homemade food, log fires and sky TV.

It was Tuesday afternoon and I thought; any port in a storm. That was until I had my hand on the front door and read the sign. Hours of opening. Friday, Saturday and Sunday. 4 p.m. – 10p.m. Oh yes, only three days to wait until the pub opens and then it doesn't open until four in the afternoon and my time off is 2 p.m. until 4 p.m.

The village shop at least was open. The fresh fruit and vegetable rack seemed to have been replenished quite soon after the war. Rotten apples, bendy carrots, the dreaded iceberg lettuce wrapped in cellophane so that it sweats and goes brown, sprouting potatoes, country fair at its worst. A newspaper or a magazine, were the only things worth buying. And even then the limited selection was depressing.

It did stop raining during the two weeks but the sheep filled field had become a bog.

I managed to convince Shaun that my calls would be diverted to his landline and that I wouldn't be on long.

Shaun was a lovely man. He had his reading by talking books, his music, occasional phone calls with friends and family and the district nurse. That was his world.

He made the best of it. I struggled to adapt to the surroundings. I know looking after a blind person should have made me feel so much happier about my own life but somehow it didn't. I was full of admiration for Shaun and here we go again, that word stoicism.

He said he hoped I would go back. I knew I wouldn't so I just said it was unlikely. It's hard to be honest in cases like that.

6. Helpful friends.

Stop her meds; she'll be dead in about 10 days.

When your client's best friend suggests that keeping her alive is going against common sense, what do you say?

I had to do a double take. I really thought Margaret Rutherford had just walked through the door.

"Here we are then." She exclaimed.

The 'we', she was referring to was her low slung sausage dog, which she had stuffed under left armpit. She carried a huge carpet bag worthy of Mary Poppins but I was guessing; she hated children. The bag was dangling from her right shoulder. I went for the bag and placed it on the floor, once I regained my balance. What did she have in there?

"Well come along. Where's the patient?"

She placed the docile pooch on the floor. It merely wondered over to where I had put the bag and lay alongside it, dragging the lead with it.

"The name's Cassandra but friends call me Cassie."

Cassie tapped me on the shoulder and nearly sent me flying.

I was mesmerized by her brown and cream brogue shoes. I worked my way up the fine oatmeal ribbed tights (which they must be, surely…not stockings)The burgundy and cream plaid skirt was bunched up around her waist, doing a wonderful job of making her look like a sack of potatoes. Her cream jumper was tucked into the skirt. Her dark brown hair was cut in an extreme short bob, with the left side hanging like a curtain over one eye. Her eyebrows had a life of their own and the crimson lipstick added an air of the Addams family to the whole charade.

Cassie alternated between flicking back the hair curtain and tugging on Bertie the dog's, lead.

I showed Cassie to her room.

"I always have this room. It has the biggest bed. We call it the gentlemen's weekend bed."

I was obviously required to ask.

"Oh, why's that?"

"So, if I have a gentleman weekend caller…" Cassie taps her nose.

I smiled and started to reassess the stocking possibility.

She obviously knew her way around so I left her to it.

I heard her enter her friend's bedroom.

"Geraldine, old girl. Still with us then?"

I suddenly wondered if Cassie had eaten and would like something to eat or drink before supper. And, okay yes I was curious to see these two together.

Cassie was giving Geraldine a bear hug.

"Said to myself. Can't believe old Gerry is going to pop her clogs but…better go and see for myself. What."

"Yep. It's true. Just been adding the final touches to my will. "

"Which you have told everyone about, naturally."

"Oooh yes." Geraldine smiled.

"Many come to your going away party?"

"Must have been fifty or so."

"Which ones were fawning all over you?"

Geraldine started to speak but Cassie cut her off.

"No. don't tell me old thing. Let me guess. The ones you will be cutting out of your will."

Raucus laughter from Geraldine.

"You know me so well."

"Ooh I wish I had been able to make it. Did you ham it up darling?"

"Certainly not. I am certifiably dying, aren't I?"

Both Cassie and Geraldine turned to me.

I nodded seriously.

"So how long then old girl? How's the pain? Want me to get a little something from my chap in…"

Cassie turns to stare at me.

I turn to leave the room but Geraldine starts laughing.

"It's okay she's one of us."

Actually I wasn't but who can deny a dying woman a bit of fun?

I muttered something about supper being in half an hour.

"Not too much for me I'm on a diet." Roared Cassie.

"A seafood diet." Chimes in Geraldine.

"Yep. I see food and I eat it."

It was obviously a well-worn, favourite joke, between the two them.

What a hoot.

Despite all the jokes, Geraldine was indeed terminally ill.

Some days she couldn't face food and other days she was ravenous but usually paid for it afterwards. They had opened her up under a general anaesthetic and sewn her back up again. Six to twelve weeks was the prognosis. The cancer was everywhere and there was nothing to be done except palliative care.

Geraldine had had a few carers, interspersed with Macmillan nurses, who do an incredible job but most of the carers just couldn't get to grips with Geraldine's philosophical attitude. It threw them and they didn't know how to react.

Let's keep it normal for as long as possible, was her wish. I could do that.

But Cassie wanted to take it a step further.

Once Gerry was tucked up for the night, her evening dose of liquid morphine would keep her comfortable for a while, Cassie said. "Come on. We need to talk."

It was my first glimpse of Gerry's best friend's serious side.

"She won't ask you but I will."

Cassie sat down heavily one of the cane kitchen chairs. It groaned under her weight.

Cassie let out an involuntary dry sob.

"She's been my best friend since prep school. We can't let her suffer."

"We are doing our best."

I didn't think she was criticising, more a case of thinking out loud.

"I know my dear. Gerry says you're being just wonderful. But she wants to start cutting back on the meds. Speed things up a bit. What do you say?"

I looked at Cassie. She was serious.

"You can't ask me to do that!"

"I mean ideally, we should stop all her meds except the morphine and she should last about ten days. Been doing a little research."

I just stared at her. Yep. She was still serious.

"Cassie, look. I do understand how you and Gerry, come to that, feel about all this but it's not that simple. I can't change any of her medication."

Cassie turned away from me. I could feel the disappointment radiating from her back.

Bertie took this moment to sidle over to his mistress. She leant down and fondled his ears.

"I know what you're going to say. We don't treat our pets as badly as our fellow humans."

Cassie turned to face me and that's a look I will never forget. All the bravado since she had arrived had evaporated and she was quietly heaving. Trying very hard to keep the tears from flowing.

"The best I can do is talk to the Macmillan nurses. We all have to stay within the law."

"Right. I'm going to bed." Cassie heaved herself out of the chair, without glancing at me and gave Bertie's lead a tug. He yelped. Not that it had been that hard a yank but he had obviously been dozing and had to re-orientate himself.

I think she knew she was being hard on me but she was desperate.

Cassie stayed for two days and she did her friend the world of good. By the time she left, Gerry was all for increasing her treatment, to see if she could last a bit longer.

That's the thing with us humans, we are capable of changing our minds. Sometimes, it can be a matter of life and death.

Gerry managed to surpass all expectations. She even considered having another going away party but she was never quite up to it. She finally threw in the towel, almost six months later. Twice as long as the best prognosis. Cassie phoned every other day but never visited again. Each time she rang she said she was somewhere different.

I've decided to travel. See all those places. You know, bucket list and all that.

I once remarked that Bettie, who I often heard in the background, must be the most, well-travelled dog. Cassie may well have been travelling but I think it was manly in her mind. It was her way of dealing with not being able to face seeing her friend for the last time.

7 You sure you know what you are doing with that syringe?

Couples can be the hardest to keep happy. They tend, subconsciously or otherwise to play one off against the other. This leaves you, the carer, as piggy in the middle. Been in that situation so often, I'm surprised I haven't sprouted a curly tale.

So there are couples and there are retired medical professionals.

With most clients, you will probably know a fair bit more about general medications/contra indications/side effects etc, than they do. However, you should always consult one of the following when there are queries. The client's GP, local pharmacy or NHS direct (by phone) and / or next of kin.

So when I was offered a two week job looking after a couple, one of whom happened to be, a retired GP. I knew I had lost the plot. I like a challenge, but really...

Fortunately the setting was idyllic. Thinking back I suppose, in their line of work, they had good pensions/savings and manage, usually, to retire somewhere half decent.

Now this house and the view from the rear had the wow factor.

It was, quite literally, perched on the south coast of England. I walked out of the enormous, ancient, verandah, suitably jungle-like, with enough climbing plants to give Kew gardens a run for its money, across the immaculately mowed, glistening green lawn, to the edge. The edge, where the lawn stopped, provided a sheer drop, down to the beach, some thirty feet below. Wow again.

It was summer and I was here for two weeks. Sorted.

What I hadn't reckoned with was the fact that retired GP was the one with Alzheimer's and not the husband as previously thought.

How do you tell a doctor that they don't know what they are doing anymore?

Very often partners will cover for their other half, not wanting to face the harsh reality. In this case the other half seemed oblivious. So it was down to the son to try and take action, except he didn't want to know.

My cause for alarm was raised when on the second day of my stay, the lady of the house, the retired GP was scurrying round the upstairs level of the house brandishing a syringe. The recipient, if she could catch him, was her husband.

Oh, yes, she's always given dad his shots. Was the son's reply. It's normal.

Well, yeah, but your mum's not normal now, is she?

More words that were never uttered.

I had no idea what the injections were for. I was groping in the dark, so to speak.

The house, the garden, the beach and the whole surrounding area was just lovely.

The husband was a sculptor and spent most of the day in his studio.

The son assured me, again, that his parents were merely eccentric. Nothing to worry about. After two days of the husband being chased by his wife I rang their GP.

Although, Mildred was no longer a practicing GP she still collected her husband's medication (the dreaded syringes) and no one seemed to have noticed her decline.

She would go to bed fully clothed. It was August, so there was no practical reason. She would get up at all times of night and make a drink in her room. Not in itself, a problem. We've all done that, but she was mixing tea with coffee and then needless to say, not drinking it.

The second morning I went into her room and she had lined up a row of empty jam jars on her dressing table. She was doing an experiment she said, with glee. I didn't dare ask what kind of experiment.

I carefully documented the last twenty four hours.

The family GP finally agreed to visit. It seemed that when they both went into the surgery, they somehow reverted to their old selves and managed to fool their way through…

He turned up unannounced, as agreed. Bingo. Neither, Mildred or her husband had any idea who he was. A phone call was made to the son and I was shipped out, with a week's pay as they both needed more qualified attention than I could give them.

Shame really but you must know your limits.

The injections were to calm …aggressive behaviour, which on the face of it, was quite ironic, as it was his wife being the aggressor. Payback, maybe?

8. You look whacked.

Go and lie down, I'll bring you a cup of tea.

It's not every day that you find yourself in a job reversal. And it has only happened once. But it was welcome and only temporary. I had had a very pleasant conversation with the daughter of the lady I was about to look after. She doesn't really need, or want, anyone but I have to be away for ten days and I would just feel so much happier knowing someone is there, looking out for her. Sounds good to me, I had responded. I had noted the use of the word want. I will do my best to make myself scarce but available, does that sound about right? The daughter had laughed and agreed. She has a very full social calendar, I'm sure you can go along with her but you may prefer some more free time. I'll leave that up to you. My mother's not a clock watcher. I just need you to be sensitive to her needs and not encroach on her independence.

Tip# 6. There are some wonderful people out there. Relish every moment.

By the time we hung up I was convinced this job was too good to be true.

Hertfordshire has some delightful villages. This was one of them.

I had just moved into my beloved cottage in Leicestershire. Not so far away and an easy drive but unpacking had taken its toll and I was shattered.

"Come in, come in. How lovely to meet you."

Roselyn said with absolute conviction, with an outstretched hand. A huge white cat strolled past the doorway, paused, glanced at Roselyn and sauntered off. I'm coming back as a pampered cat in my next life. Either that or a tall man.

"You can park in the yard. Save moving it later."

Roselyn, the thoughtful client.

The five bar gate was open so I drove into the gravel yard. A courtyard to be precise with what looked like stables on three sides. Her daughter hadn't mentioned horses but you never knew what people could deem unnecessary to tell you. As long as I didn't have to do anything with them. I know people rave about them but in my experience they can be dangerous at both ends. Maybe I'll come back as a tall gay man who loves horses.

The top half of a stable door suddenly flew open to my right.

Roselyn's head appeared. "Cup of tea?"

"Oh, yes please."

"Take your bags through the front door, up the stairs and your room is on the right. Go and unpack and I'll bring your cup of tea up to you. You look shattered my dear!"

I had explained to Roselyn's daughter that I had just moved house but she may not have told her mother.

"No, honestly, I'll come down."

"No, won't hear of it. Now scoot."

Okay, so at this point I was thinking, she likes to sleep walk naked or eat with her mouth open, or puts her hands down the toilet. Yep, seen them all. She just seemed too good to be true . I was hoping for a couple of regular clients now that I had moved into a cottage that I couldn't quite afford. I kept my fingers mentally crossed as I unpacked. My bedroom was quintessentially chintz. A page out of country living magazine, courtesy of Colefax and Fowler. Even the bedspread matched the curtains. Tiny floral pattern on a cream background. There was even a stand with a porcelain wash bowl and jug. Cream towels and a flannel had been laid out on my bed. I always sit down on the edge of the bed with trepidation. Too soft and I would get backache. Too hard and I wouldn't get any sleep at all. At least having a car meant bringing your own pillow, so that was no problem.

A gentle tap on the door and there was Roselyn with my tray. Tea and shortbread. I could cry.

"Frances told me you had just moved house. It was good of you to come at such short notice."

"Not at all. She assured me that you would not be heavy duty."

Roselyn gave a gentle but genuine laugh. "Oh, I won't be any trouble. I promise."

"Now, you drink your tea and come down in time for the six o clock news. How does that sound?"

"Perfect. Thank you."

"Beautiful room…" I started to say but Roselyn had retreated leaving the door slightly ajar.

I went downstairs at ten to six.

"Ah good. You feel better?" Roselyn smiled at me and patted the squidgy, old, floral overstuffed armchair next to hers.

I sank down into it and my feet came up. It was a recliner. I could get used to this.

"Now I know what you are supposed to do and indeed what I am paying you for but do I look like I need a carer?"

Uh-oh. This could be tricky.

I opened my mouth and closed it again.

Roselyn had her hand in the air.

"Just hear me out, ok?"

You may prefer some free time. I'll leave that up to you. I was recalling what her daughter had said.

For once there seemed to be agreement between the client and their family.

"You usually have two hours free time each afternoon. Am I correct?"

I nodded.

"Well I would like you to have each afternoon off. Or the morning or we could alternate according to my plans. So you would have, say, two until five thirty or nine until twelve thirty. How does that sound? And in the evenings if we happen to want to watch the same programme all well and good but otherwise I really do prefer to be myself. Your room is comfortable I think and the television is up to date and the radio works. And there are enough books lining the walls along the landing to start a library. What do you say?"

"You sure you only, erm, *don't need me,* for two weeks. I could stay longer."

Roselyn gave a nervous cough and a sigh of relief at the same time which developed into a strange coughing spasm.

Of course that was the moment the phone rang.

Roselyn was waving her hand in front of her. We all do it and yet it never actually helps.

Roselyn leaped up and dashed into the kitchen, pointing to me to lift the receiver at the same time.

"Good evening, Miss Chadwick's residence."

I heard Roselyn start to splutter as she gulped down some water.

Oh heck that was the last client.

"Laura, is that you? Have you forgotten where you are already?"

"I'm so sorry. Only a momentary lapse it won't happen again. Yes, yes, your mother is absolutely fine. She was just in the cloakroom. Here she is."

I handed the receiver over to Roselyn, who winked at me.

I went into the kitchen to discover she had laid out two trays.

A casserole was gently warming in the oven.

I didn't even have to cook, not tonight anyway.

I went in search of the larder and some fresh vegetables, straight from the garden.

Beyond the larder was another room. It had a stable door so I opened the top half.

Ooh. That looked interesting. A kiln.

Our Roselyn was the creative type. Brilliant.

We chatted easily over supper. We both liked the Channel Four news and then we went our separate ways.

At nine pm I went downstairs to ask Roselyn, if she liked a bedtime story with her cocoa.

She picked up the cushion on the adjacent chair and threw it at me.

I took that as a no.

Ten days later I returned to my cottage, with an assortment of hand painted pottery. All the work of my own fair hands. It's very rare to get such a self-sufficient client and one that teaches you a new skill into the bargain.

9. A Mouse in the Vinaigrette

Schloop…plop. Schloop…plop.

You think by the time you reach forty you must have heard pretty much every household sound. Cisterns fizzing and filling, bacon sizzling, refrigerators humming, clocks tick, ticking, like a heartbeat in the home. But, schloop...plop? Nope, my auditory repertoire was not registering, and believe me, my ears work well; handy in my line of work.

It was my first assignment and the lady turned out to be the wonderfully warm grandmotherly type. It was a rambling eight bedroom house, acres of garden and my first Aga. And that was where I stood stirring the porridge in an original Le Creuset saucepan, my wooden spoon performing a figure of eight just the way we had been taught at school, when I heard this weird sound.

My first Aga. It still elicits a fond sigh as the memory pops into my head. If you have ever done toast on a hotplate you will have used what I can only describe as one of those hinged double tennis racket contraptions that hold the bread in place on the heat. I was flipping my first piece of toast and stirring porridge at the same time. Multi tasking at 8am in a strange kitchen. I had heard that you can leave porridge overnight to cook in the bottom oven but I didn't want to risk encrusted oats, a washing up nightmare on my first morning.

Ignoring the ongoing sound I happily placed a bowl of porridge, toast, now released from its criss-cross cage, crusts cut off, cut into triangles and placed in a silver toast rack on a tray that was courtesy of the diary of an English country woman, which in turn was almost obliterated by a linen tray cloth, hand embroidered, silver cruet (at all times) cut glass honey pot with yellow and black china lid, containing lime marmalade and the marmalade spoon, the one with the lip near the top of the handle. A white porcelain shell shaped dish for the butter curls. Butter was kept in the larder for easier curling. A small white jug, embossed with minute pink flowers for the milk and a silver sugar bowl containing light Muscuvado sugar. A dessert spoon for the porridge, a small knife for the toast, a teaspoon for the...aah, coffee. So that's what I could hear. The coffee had been perking away behind me for some time. It was the sort that you plugged in, put cold water in the bottom and coffee granules in the top filter, bit like one of those science experiments you did at school when you watched to see which way the liquid would go and what would be the end result. Now which was the right coffee cup to use for breakfast?? Mrs B had gone over all these details last night but now I was blowed if I could remember.

Tip #7. If you think you may forget. Lay the breakfast tray/table the night before while it is still fresh in your mind.

And lastly, often most importantly, the starched linen napkin complete with correct silver napkin ring. Using the deceased husband's napkin ring is not recommended especially on the first day. You will often find personal items such as shaving brush, gardening shoes, dog leads in the house even though husbands and pets are long departed. So, never assume...always check before offering to take the dog for a walk etc.

I once grabbed the wrong (i.e. deceased husband's) dressing gown to put round the shoulders of a lady in the middle of the night. She had woken up having an angina attack which brings to mind the fine line between helping and hindrance. She said nothing at the time but was very forgiving once she thought about it.

A sudden vision of my new charge sitting up in bed, arms folded, hands in armpits, pin curl clips still nestling either side of her temples and a pained expression on her face as she stares wilfully at the bedroom door, almost catapulted me out of the door. Not a good idea when carrying a tray. So I did a final check. Agh! Butter knife...small rounded end, dinky cream coloured handle (don't ask, probably extinct now).

All present and correct.

I needn't have worried. If Mrs B had been wide awake, she feigned rousing herself, brilliantly. In fact over the next two weeks I was to discover an attitude to life, a philosophy even; that stays with me even today. I was truly lucky to have her as my guinea pig!

To get from the kitchen to the main bedroom would seem an easy task but with three doors leading from the kitchen...perhaps I should design a clip on Sat Nav (to your apron, naturally) so you can find your way round your new 'home'!

Across the hall to the stairs of course is simple but once on the landing you have five doors one way and ten the other. Now if you have been paying attention you will be thinking, she said eight bedrooms. True. But some bedrooms have two doors and then there are three bathrooms, store cupboards, laundry rooms, and winter wardrobes. As a rule of thumb, if there are back stairs, the ladies' bedroom won't be in that direction.

For some reason I had anticipated this problem and left my bedroom door open which was next to Mrs B's and saved fumbling with creaky doorknobs. Ta dah!

She told me to have my breakfast, take my time and come back for the tray when I was ready. She had nothing urgent to do today...she said. I was soon to discover that her short term memory was her one failing. We soon got a system going whereby she called me to write in her diary if anyone phoned. She made a joke out of a rotten situation.

"My social secretary will have a word with you. My diary is so full you understand." She had many friends and they all did.

As I opened the door to the cellar I realised that the door *next* to it, was the way into the kitchen I had come down the backstairs and therefore can be forgiven for getting mislaid, I won't say lost, far too dramatic.

I sat at the old oak kitchen table with my porridge eating it with any old spoon but definitely muscovado sugar, a lady of taste, both of us! I looked up at the old wood and glass rectangular box above the door that had the name of the main rooms in the house. The push button bell in the drawing room still worked I was later to find out. The name would sway and tinkle, summoning staff to the designated room.

I started to wonder how long this lady and her family had lived in this wonderful house. It had a very welcoming, homely feel to it.

I poured myself a cup of coffee; was going to have a mug and then thought, no it's more in keeping with my surroundings.

I had switched off the coffee percolator before I had taken the tray upstairs. The coffee was still hot *and* silent. But there it was again, that peculiar sound. I'd left the porridge pan on the side of the Aga and was about to fill it with hot water ready for washing when I came eyeball to eyeball with my first of many encounters with mice. Only this one seemed to have strayed right out of a cartoon. The Aga was built into a recess that no doubt once housed an open fireplace and sensibly worktops had been arranged on either side. Somehow I hadn't noticed at the far left hand corner there was a jam jar with homemade vinaigrette in it. However this particular one had extra flavour, in the shape of a mouse. A real live mouse that was trying desperately to extricate itself from this greasy concoction. He (I have to assume it was male!) could manage to get his head, sleeked down, 1950's style, above the rim of the jar, whiskers twitching frantically but he was obviously exhausted and couldn't pull himself up any further, hence the schloop, coming up and the plop when he sank back down. Now, along with most people's views, mice are not my favourite creatures but can you imagine how absurdly tragic this situation was! I guessed it would take a while to deal with so I decided on going to retrieve Mrs B's tray before starting on my rescue mission.

The lady in question was just getting out of bed when I entered her room. She told me that she would be doing her toilette, getting her clothes out for the day and then she would do her yoga exercises. Mrs B was 92 years old. So when she asked me if everything was ok and had I found everything I needed in the kitchen, I expect she thought that my expression, somewhere between Eric Morecombe singing Bring me Sunshine and someone knowing they have a lottery ticket with the winning numbers on it...somewhere… was due to her explaining that she needed the cushions from the chair to help her with her shoulder stands.

She asked me to come back in half an hour to 'supervise' her bath. "I know what to do but my children fear I may forget and drown." This was typical of her gentle wit and we soon fell into a comfortable liaison. I told her towards the end of my stay about Brylcreme Jerry and she roared with laughter but I couldn't imagine, on my first morning saying. "Yes, everything is fine but do you usually have a mouse in your vinaigrette?"

I loaded the dishwasher, pans and all and set about releasing my slippery friend.

It was a mild spring day so it seemed like a plan to take the jar outside, lay it on its side and let the mouse and vinaigrette run out. I laid it on the edge of the grass pointing into a flower bed. I thought the path would become slippery and dangerous. For humans not the mouse! I decided the poor thing must be terrified so rather than give the jam jar bottom a whack I just left it to slither out. Five minutes past and I was worried that if Mrs B called me I wouldn't hear.

"C'mon, you daft bugger, out you come."

I was leaning over the flower bed concentrating on Jerry's bid for freedom and didn't hear someone approaching from the back of the shed.

The agency had mentioned a gardener but you never take it all in at first.

"Jeez!" I jumped as a deep male Gloucester voice said. "This should help."

The gardener, who bizarrely was called, Gerry was brandishing a hammer.

"No" I yelled. Suffocated by oil and vinegar and then to be showered by fragments of broken glass. I didn't think so. Somewhere between being scared of mice and feeling sorry for Jerry (always bad idea to name them) I had become Mouse Savers International.

"Okay," he shrugged and wandered back down the garden. I quickly went in doors to get...what...for heaven's sake? Seeing as Jerry was trying to launch himself from his glass womb I suddenly thought, ah, tongs...a forceps delivery. I was about to grab the cooking tongs, I could always put them in the dishwasher afterwards when I spotted an old pair of wooden washing tongs hanging up by the larder door. Perfect, much gentler. My thirty minutes was nearly up so I dashed outside. The jam jar was still intact but it was facing the opposite direction and was empty. I had wondered if I should take some washing up liquid to cut through some of the grease but decided Jerry would probably not be up for the idea. As it was, he was nowhere to be seen.

I'll never know what happened to my slippery friend and the schloop- plop sound is one that I haven't heard from that day to this, I'm glad to say.

Talking of sounds. A word of warning. If you're at all nosey and I don't mean going through cupboards, just things that are in plain view as they say on all the best TV cop dramas, beware of a wonderfully carved inlaid wooden box on the landing at 11pm. Remember you are not auditioning for the Antiques Road Show or Cash in the Attic. Curious though you may be, have you any idea just how loud a musical box can sound at that time of night?!

10. Midnight chocolate nibbler.

There are many things you remember about people you have looked after. With this particular client, the first thing that comes to mind is her voice. It was tiny. She was large and this made it even more surprising. I don't mean she was fat, just big boned, matronly but in a motherly way. She had a bosom as opposed to any other kind of female appendages. She could rest her cup and saucer quite safely on it, when she sat down.

She wore a range of 1950's frocks with tiny, pre-Laura Ashley type prints. They were often pinched in at the waist, well halfway between the sweetheart neckline and the hem, with a narrow leather belt, picking out one of the colours from the pattern. Mrs M had a mass of white hair, which she had set once a week at the local hairdresser's. I always tried to keep quiet about my previous life. *Ooh you're a hairdresser, as well. Ooh, I'll cancel my appointments for the next two weeks.* This could go one of two ways. The client hates the way you do her hair and sulks, which is awkward as you live 'together' or, as did happen once, they love the way you do their hair so much, they insist on being driven to their usual hairdresser so that can see what they have been doing wrong, all these years. Great.

Mrs M wore lily of the valley perfume and really belonged in a bygone era. She seemed to waft from room to room. She was amazingly graceful for such a large lady. She had rosy cheeks which turned quite burgundy if she felt she had said something slightly risqué.

She used to have a dog. A white 'Scottie'. Angus, she called him. But once her hip started giving her gip, she felt it unfair to keep him as she couldn't take him for the nice long walks that he really needed. She gave a wry smile as she emphasized the word needed. He was a little devil if he didn't get his proper exercise.

The kitchen however was ultramodern. Every gadget you could think of. Electric and otherwise.

Breadmakers, icecream makers, yoghurt makers and a newly acquired expresso machine.

I was soon to discover that the latter had been bought by one of her sons as a Christmas present.

Mrs M only drank tea.

The only time I ever heard her grumble, she was otherwise unfailingly nice about everybody, was about her sons. They are not bad boys but I do wish I had had a daughter. Daughters listen, she used to say.

Three sons in the UK and not one of them came to visit more than once a year.

Two had grandchildren. There were photos everywhere. The grand piano, her husband used to play, is host to at least thirty photographs. She dusted them and replaced them in exactly the same positions, religiously once a week.

Mrs M had a cleaner but the piano was off limits.

She also had a gardener and a regular handyman who would come at a moment's notice. She had a plethora of friends in the town and they did the rounds. Coffee mornings, bridge parties, church fairs and concerts. But somehow, she didn't seem to have any close friends and yet she seemed the kindest, gentlest lady you could wish to meet.

Mrs M was recovering from a hip replacement when I went to her. The hip itself had healed perfectly but she had been feeling, below par, even to the point of saying she was a little down. See, it's that stoicism again. Mustn't grumble. Feeling depressed but musn't use that word. No way.

It was one of her sons who contacted me and said a friend of the family had recommended me. I had been to Newbury many times, particularly the ring road...It goes around and around.

It is a pleasant enough town but doesn't grab me in the way that Salisbury does, for example. A city with the heart of a village. Perfect. But I digress.

Mrs M's son explained that although his mother was back on her feet, she wasn't quite 'back on her feet'. Oh the joys of the English language. He thought he was so clever and funny. I immediately said I understood the dilemma and the joke. I have looked after a few people who have had extensive surgery and most times the physical side goes according to plan but often people are unprepared for the feelings of doom and gloom that sets in. I was to stay with Mrs M for two weeks to help her regain her joie de vivre. Her son insisted that she used to have one. Another one of his little jokes. Maybe it was as well, he stayed away.

I have to confess I much prefer to go shopping alone but as Mrs M needed to restore her confidence, driving and shopping would be a good place to start. Working in England is something I have been doing for most of my life and there are two things that ease the 'pain'. Reasonable proximity to the two W's. Waitrose and Waterstones. The first because I know I can get fruit and vegetables that will be edible when you get home, not next week, and that's if you catch the products at the critical moment between hard and bad. And Waterstones for obvious reasons.

Mrs M assured me that both were available. So, to recap, I have a lovely lady, not demanding. Very comfortable house. A cleaner and a gardener. One of the good assignments. Mrs M had been living off 'ready meals' and they were not too bad, she said but nothing beats the smell of a home cooked meal. I totally agreed.

I managed to persuade Mrs M that she should drive as it would be easier than directing me. She said she would drive there and I could drive back. Deal. A Honda automatic. As easy as sitting in an armchair on wheels.

It was only three miles to the supermarket but the speed restrictions meant that Mrs M could not give 'the old girl', as she referred to her car, a bit of wellie. An expression I had not heard in a long time and I certainly didn't expect from her.

Another expression, dark horse, came to mind at that moment. I was going to enjoy getting to know this client.

We stocked up on assortment of vegetables, fish and meat. Some of which Mrs M said she had never eaten. What! Never had sweet potato with fennel and fresh salmon but she was willing to try.

As I was unloading the shopping Mrs M said she had a confession to make. I knew it! Well. No, I didn't know what it was, just that there was more to her than met the eye.

"I'm supposed to watch my diet. I'm borderline diabetic."

She said with a look of gloom that I hadn't seen before.

"Ah," I said, as I unpacked the muscavado sugar.

Now you tell me.

"And my cholesterol is a little high...." she tailed off, plonking down in one of the cane kitchen chairs. Her ampleness, flowed either side of the chair.

"I used to be a size 14," she sighed.

"Now come on, you've been inactive for what two months, with this hip of yours and you could hardly do much exercise before that could you, what with the pain etc. So you're bound to have suffered all around really."

"But you like everything, as far as you know, and we can make some delicious salads and the doctor says you must start walking more. Come on, as soon as I have put this lot away we will make a plan. Menus and exercise. Ok."

I glanced across to see a single tear rundown Mrs M's cheek. My back had been turned as I had been mainly shifting my focus from shopping bags to larder shelves, and now I stopped.

"Hey," I said, putting an arm round her shoulders.

"Summer's round the corner and we can skip Easter, next weekend. Who needs chocolate anyway?"

At this Mrs M started to sob.

Oh boy.

"A drop of sherry and a chocolate truffle. It's a not a lot to ask is it?"

She looked at me imploringly.

I was going to have my work cut out.

The next morning we drew up a list. Lots of soups, homemade, naturally. Salads and fruit. We'd both cut out cheese and chocolate for a week and see what happened. We made a pact.

No chocolate for a week didn't present too much of a problem for me. It was far harder to ignore the cheese craving. I suggested we didn't weigh ourselves for a week. A daily weigh-in can be so depressing and we had enough of that going round.

Mrs M liked to hear about my travels and I enjoyed sharing her photo albums. We soon got into a comfortable routine. By the end of the first week, we had a celebratory drink. Mrs M had a dry sherry. I had a ginger wine. So many calories…

The weigh-in proved successful, we had lost 5 lbs between us.

The following two days, I was presented with a dilemma. Mrs M's mood had lifted considerably, which was great. Just shows what a little TLC can do but I wondered how to tackle the fact that Mrs M seemed to be, well, cheating. The last few mornings I had seen the evidence.

Next to the oats, in the pantry were some slabs of dark chocolate. As I got the oats out ready to make our porridge I couldn't help but notice, two of the three chocolate slabs had been opened at one end and some of the chocolate, nibbled away.

But she had lost some weight. So maybe I should go easy on her…

It was more the, borderline diabetes that bothered me.

It was no good I was going to have to say something.

We finished a hearty breakfast of kiwi fruit, eaten, boiled egg style and porridge with a little honey instead of sugar. I had agreed that plain porridge was prison food.

We had both cut sugar in tea and coffee. It was a good start.

I looked at Mrs M as she drained her coffee cup.

"Why are you looking at me like that?"

Mrs M dabbed at her chin with her linen napkin.

"Is that better?"

"No, I mean it's nothing to do with your face."

Mrs M puckered up her lips.

"You're not leaving are you?"

"No, no. Nothing like that. Look, we've both been doing really well with this diet thing. Wouldn't you say?"

"Yes. It's been easier than I thought. Thanks to you."

"Hmm. No problem. It's good for me too but…oh heck I'm just going to say it."

"What?"

"Have you been cheating…just a little bit?"

Mrs M looked thoughtful.

"Have I? I don't thinks so. Why?"

I went into the pantry and brought out the evidence.

I put the two chocolate bars on the breakfast table, between us.

Mrs M picked one up and turned it over. Then she started to laugh.

"You thought…Come with me."

She grabbed hold of my hand and led me back into the pantry.

Mrs M pointed to the floor. The corner directly below the shelf with the chocolate.

"Mice, Laura. We have mice!"

"Oh good grief. How foolish am I?"

"Well, yes and no. You weren't to know we had a mouse problem in here. Didn't want to frighten you away. The gardener assured me he had got rid of them. Obvioulsy not."

We sat back at the breakfast table.

Mrs M started to laugh again.

"But you make a lousy detective." She held up the end of the chocolate bar, in front of her mouth. "Just how small do you think my teeth are?"

I had to agree. I hadn't thought of that.

The nibbles were very delicate…

The rest of my stay was punctuated by Mrs M suddenly raising the backs of both hands, mouse-like and twitching her mouth. It did her the world of good…to have something to laugh about.

I aim to please.

11   The Spirit of Christmas.

It was four forty five a.m. when Doris suddenly announced that she felt able to make the transit from armchair to her upstairs bed. It was five fifteen a.m. when I called the paramedics. I am so grateful to who ever invented cordless phones, it meant I could sit with Doris perched halfway up the stairs until help arrived.

"I'm not being much help am I?" I said.

"No." she said "But your smile goes a long way."

It was one of the nicest things that anyone has ever said to me. Thank you Doris. The paramedics got her into bed. Doris would not go to hospital. At eight a.m. I rang her GP. Doris had a urine infection and it was the twenty third of December.

Doris like me has no children. And next of kin is about two hundred miles away. I duly informed her of our plight. When I say I our, I meant mine, quite frankly. Doris although normally in charge of all her faculties could not remember the pin numbers for her bank card and there was no money in the house. When you're living- in as a carer/ housekeeper, part of the deal is that you get fed and watered. So it seemed that my ever expanding credit card would have to be used until after Christmas when a cheque could be arranged. All Doris's finances were organized by her solicitor who was away until the third of January. Hey ho.

Money aside, poor Doris was about to spend Christmas in hospital with me visiting daily which meant a twenty minute walk to the train station then after that a fifteen minute bus ride. (Two years later a girl was murdered on that route to the station.)

The ambulance came for Doris at eleven thirty. I went with her. Doris had given up her car two years before. She hated losing her independence but after removing her neighbour's wing mirror for the second time in ten days, she decided that if she couldn't even swing into her own driveway it was time to give up.

Doris was admitted at midday on the twenty third of December with a urine infection but she still had her wits about her. After sitting in a cubicle for about an hour both Doris and I were startled when a young nurse appeared, throwing back the curtains, metal rings grating on a metal pole and sat down, clipboard in hand. She asked all the same questions that the nurse had asked when we arrived. Double checking I suppose but very irritating for Doris.

Nurse. "Doris, may I call you Doris? (No pause for Doris to reply) Do you know the name of this hospital?"

Doris. "My dear girl, how long have you worked here and you don't know the name of this place?"

I mentally high-fived Doris.

I hated leaving Doris in that place. Once she was on the ward and settled they would do further tests and I could ring later to find out the results. So I duly made my way back to my home for the next few days. Of course I knew Doris's address and I had arrived by train and taxi, only the day before but from a different direction so with no car and no sat nav I took the shuttle bus from the hospital to the station. It's normal practice to take a taxi to and from your clients at the beginning and the end of the booking mainly because you usually have too much luggage but somehow I didn't feel this occasion warranted the expense mine, or Doris's. It was getting dark and the pavements were still icy but looking at the map in the station it looked like a very straightforward route if I cut across the park. In my next life and coming back as a tall man (great for supermarket shelves and peeing) with a fabulous sense of direction. As I put the key into Doris's front door I had the feeling that someone else had been in the house, not in a scary way more a comforting way really.

As a true Brit the first thing I did was put the kettle on. When all else fails as Tony Hancock used to say: Tea, tea, is that your answer to everything? Well at this moment in time, yes! Holding a cup of Earl Grey in one hand I lifted the phone to inform Doris's niece, Paula of her plight. I thought about mentioning the lack of money but it seemed inappropriate somehow. I explained that I would phone as soon as I had any further results. She thanked me profusely and said have a good night's rest, you deserve it.

The first night in any house is strange. Sights are easy to deal with, you close your eyes but sounds and smells permeate the moments or even hours before sleep. Central heating boilers spring to life, pipes rattling, and all too often, the smell of damp, in English houses. This one was no exception. I had already moved my bed so that my head was not directly below a bulge in the ceiling which looked as if it may deposit damp plaster on my head at any moment.

I phoned the hospital at nine p.m and they said. *Doris is comfortable. Ring* tomorrow. Did I believe them? Did I heck! I managed to sleep quite well probably due to a complete lack of sleep the night before even managing not to fall out of the single bed.

"Visiting two till four." Was all I got when I rang to enquire about Doris.

It would take me about an hour to get back to the hospital so I had time to go and buy myself a small Christmas feast. Fortunately I already knew where the local shops were. Always one of my first enquiries, along with where are the fuse box and the stop cock? Believe me I have needed them both on more than one occasion.

It was ten a.m when I ventured out and a watery sun was attempting to make the pavements passable. You can picture it. Christmas Eve in a small Surrey village; quintessentially English. Men scurrying, scarf clad, nose- dripping children, tugging at adults coats pointing at shop windows. A plethora of four by fours swoosh through the melted snow; pavement dwellers beware. This village not big enough for Tesco's had a small but perfectly formed Co-op. And they actually do a decent goat's cheese so all was not lost. So, what do you buy for Christmas lunch for one when you're on a budget? Of course frozen chicken tikka masala and Nan bread and mince pies and a ridiculous priced mango but then it had flown halfway round the world. My carbon footprint just escalated but then I don't have a car so that's OK then. Laden with four carrier bags... What have I bought? I didn't notice their weight until I reached the end of the shops, where the houses began.

A very respectable, Barbour clad, middle aged man stood outside in the last shop, a charity shop I think, he was holding a collecting tin with a Round Table written on it. Had he been selling the Big Issue I would have stopped. I always buy it; nothing altruistic you understand, simply the fact I feel I may end up selling it myself one day so I buy it as a kind of insurance. I gave the man a slight shrug as I walked past him as if to say, sorry all my money is in these carrier bags. I counted down the houses only ten more to go but boy, my arms were aching so I put the bags down on the pavement for a moment and leant against someone's hedge. I jumped as the middle aged voice came from behind me.

"Can I help you with those?" It was the man with the collecting tin which was now under his arm. I blinked and considered his question. This was not New York, why did I think he was going to run off with my shopping? As I still hadn't answered his question he tried another.

"Do you have far to go?"

"No, only number 23 thanks."

I saw a kindly gentleman he saw a stubborn feminist. We both smiled at the same time, maybe reading each other's thoughts.

"Number 23" he said. "So you're looking after Doris?"

"If only..." I said. And then the whole story poured out, of course.

He lived in an adjacent street and had known Doris and Bill for many years.

What a couple, he said. Like teenagers right up until the day he died and Doris well, don't you worry she'll pull through.

George deposited my four carrier bags on Doris's front doorstep and bade me goodbye.

Halfway down the drive the kind gentleman turned back and said. "Will you be okay?"

"Fine," I said "Really; this has happened before." I gave him my most reassuring smile.

"Give my best to Doris when you see her later. I'm George, wife's name is Jane," he said.

I'm sure he could see me thinking what was his name again? I devoured a nice piece of fresh salmon with spinach and potatoes for lunch. Got to keep my strength up. I had just finished when there was a knock at the door. Word had probably got around about Doris. I've found villages can be quite good like that.

"Ah George, hello."

"Something smells nice," he said.

"Yes, just had an early lunch, off to see Doris soon in hospital."

"Oh yes I would take you, but I can't today."

"Please don't worry this is all part and parcel of what I do."

"Okay," said George looking a little more comfortable. "Now what I am about to say is a statement not a question okay?" He says he's very forcibly but with a huge smile. "You will come and spend Christmas day with us. I will pick you up at eleven thirty and my son will bring you home around six o clock. He is designated driver."

I opened my mouth to protest.

George raised the index finger of his right hand." No. He has to take his grandmother home anyway and she's round the corner, so no problem. Okay? "

"Is that a statement or a question?" I said laughing. George simply raised his eyebrows.

"If you walk to the station while it's lights that's fine but please get a taxi back. Doris may not remember to say it but it is what she would want you to do."

Doris was sitting up in the leafing through a glossy magazine when I arrived. She didn't look at all well but what could you expect? I always hate leaving people in hospital but reckoned Doris could hold her own. She absolutely insisted that I didn't go in the next day. Christmas day there'll be no buses and taxis will charge an arm and a leg. Then I told her about George.

"Room for one more at the Inn," she winked. "They are a lovely family. Jane works with autistic children, music therapy I think; something like that. You have a good time."

I had taken flowers and fruit and magazines, this was back when all those were allowed in hospital.

As I turned to leave Doris said, "In the pantry you'll find a bottle of vintage port. Blow off the dust and take that tomorrow."

When you're living in somebody else's house it is tempting to nose beyond what you can actually see, but I try to live by the adage ' do as you would be done by' and so usually, I just can't do it. If things are in plain view as they say on all the best American TV cop programmes, then fine. Family photos, cards, books; all fascinating. I can almost hear Lloyd Grossman saying 'And who lives in a house like this?' So many photos of a very happy Doris and Bill. I wondered how long it had been since he died? As I was thinking this I was opening the door to a room that I hadn't discovered yet. It was off the hall, next to the downstairs loo but I had no idea what the room was used for. Before I had chance to take in my surroundings I realized I could smell cigar smoke. It stopped me in my tracks. I surveyed the room with its prominent oak desk and even more prominent black and white photograph of Doristhi in a ball gown circa 1920s. Wow!

The room felt as if it was still in use. Somehow felt different to the rest of the house as if someone had hit the pause button. I broke my own rules as I was compelled to open the top left hand drawer of the desk. A silver cigar cutter and a small opaque paperweight. I smiled as the smell of cigar smoke drifted away. The phone rang so I dashed into the hall pick it up. It was Paula, Doris's niece.

"Has Doris left you with any money?" This was her opening gambit.

"Well no actually but don't worry I'll sort it out after Christmas." Then I told her about George and my Christmas day invite.

"Ah," she said. "The spirit of Christmas is not dead then, I'm so glad."

I had the best Christmas day I'd had in years surrounded by strangers, all happy in each other's company, laughing, including me, I never felt for one moment out of place. They were all in stitches when I told them I had bought a chicken tikka masala.

"But that's Boxing Day food!" Their youngest grandson told me.

In between crackers, jokes and silly hats, I asked Jane to tell me something about Doris and Bill. She told me Bill had died 10 years earlier. He had been cycling into the village for his daily exercise to get the newspaper so he could do the crossword to keep his mind fit, when a delivery van reversed out of a side road. Bill had no chance. Doris had pleaded with Bill to give up cigars, she was worried lung cancer would see him off.

"Nope, more likely to get run down by a bus!" This was always Bill's reply. Through all her tears and sadness she could see the irony and his headstone reads: *You were almost right. Miss you morning, noon and night but I know you are still with me. God bless.*

I went to see Doris every day. There was little improvement. I spoke to the solicitor on the third of January who was devastated at the dilemma her absence had caused. She transferred my money and expenses directly into my account. I rang Paula before I left, to ask if I could ring to find out how Doris was doing in the next week or so. Paula assured me she was arriving at the hospital with the fringe on top that very afternoon. I rang Paula ten days later. She had moved Doris into a private hospital where she had blood tests, a blood transfusion, and a new lease of life. She was now at home having only help twice a day.

"Oh and a message from Doris. She said you were to keep smiling and you would know what it meant.

12   Taps and tackle.

I knew this was going to be a tricky one, couples always are.

It was the man who needed care as his wife was finding it increasingly difficult to cope. It was a very large bungalow in about one acre of Hertfordshire countryside. I parked my car in between the garage and the kitchen door. At least I think that's where it was.

I walked round to the front door and was immediately greeted by a very tall elegant woman with white, short cropped hair. She extended her hand and bade me come in.

Her husband appeared behind her in his self- propelled wheelchair. He was the male carbon copy of her. Never have I seen such an obvious couple. This seemed like a good start.

Jessica had suggested I bring my things from the car via the laundry room, kitchen and into the hall. All fairly straightforward even with my sense of direction. As I appeared in the hallway laden with too many bags, they both smiled. Jonathan pointed to the stair lift in this dormer bungalow. I would be sleeping upstairs. That at least would give them both a little more privacy.

With my bags upstairs and a nod to myself that this job wouldn't be so bad after all, I went downstairs to start lunch.

"Let us just have a salad, nice and easy for you."

In England of the course, this usually means a slice of ham, half a tomato and lettuce leaf and not much else. Unless you count one slice of bread and butter.

Jonathan and Jessica had made very good uses of their one acre.

They had one of the best vegetable gardens I'd seen in a long time.

Opening the, not really cold enough, fridge door, true to form Jessica pointed to four, slimy slices of ham in a plastic packet.

"Would you like to help yourself to a lettuce from the garden and there should be several tomatoes ripe in the greenhouse."

"Any beetroot," I ventured?

They both look puzzled and then shook their heads.

This was not going to be a gourmet fortnight.

I managed to extract the lettuce with the aid of a kitchen knife and I wondered if I dare suggest a nice, light vinaigrette?

Better keep on safe ground for the first 24 hours. No doubt there would be a bottle of salad cream lurking in the pantry the top being encrusted, never having been wiped. But I couldn't let the foibles of English country living get to me. One had work to do and one was being paid.

I took the lettuce and tomatoes, courtesy of a wooden basket into the laundry room where there was a nice big stainless steel sink. After a while you start to realise what to expect. This looks like the kind of house that would have a salad spinner/ dryer/thingy.

Putting the salad on the draining board I turned on the cold water and put in the plug. A simple enough task, unless the aforementioned tap comes away in your hand and as this particular sink was fed directly from the mains, it had excellent pressure and now cold water was shooting up and hitting the ceiling. Great...

"Erm, Jessica, I'm afraid..."

I didn't need to continue, Jessica had obviously heard the rush of water.

Jonathon had strong wrists but being wheelchair bound he was unable to reach underneath the sink and turn off the stop cock. Neither Jessica nor I could turn the damn thing. As luck would have it, the doorbell rang and the milkman, only here to collect his weekly money was swiftly ushered into the laundry room.

It took him a couple of attempts but he managed to stop the flow.

"Now you see Jonathan, what I have been saying all these weeks. Things needs doing. They don't just happen. They have to be arranged."

Oh great, my favourite. A couple's argument. You can usually tell which one is going to win from the outset. But this time I wasn't so sure.

They seemed to have forgotten all about me until I said. "I'm really sorry I have no idea how that happened. I'm generally not that strong."

They both turned to look at me. I swear they really had forgotten I was there. Curious.

I was dismissed after an uneventful lunch and told to make myself at home, take a nap, walk in the garden (it had started to rain) and reappear whenever I wanted.

Tip #8. They don't mean it. Break time is two hours, no more and if you're wise, no less.

I felt like a snooze but wasn't sure that the combination of a tasteless ham salad and tinned peaches for afters... yum ;-(would stay down.

I didn't feel sick exactly but just decidedly queasy.

You really can't afford to be fussy in this line of work but I am very sensitive to smells. Unfortunately my new bedroom had one. An indistinct but persistent pong. I couldn't put my finger on it. I had to remind myself that although not far from the town of Ware in Hertfordshire (wonderful fodder for stupid phone calls with friends...you're where? Yes...) This dormer bungalow was decidedly in the country. So, just good healthy, country smells. Yes, that was it. I'd soon get used to it. I flung the window open as far as it would go and stuck my head out. Nope the smell was definitely emanating from inside the room.

I had to take myself in hand and refrain from doing a guest version of Fawlty Towers.

Me: I say... do you have another room? This one smells!

No, not an option. I unpacked my case and soon had the scented candle alight that I had learned was a necessity for me in some places.

And yes, for all you health and safety freaks (I am one) I never leave the candle unattended. I had tried various air fresheners over the years but they didn't do the job for long enough.

I got used to the bedroom over a couple of nights. And in the end they turned out to be one of the easier couples to look after. But we had to make one or two changes for this to happen.

Jonathan needed a lot of help as he was confined to a wheelchair and needed help with washing and toileting. Most men are understandably anxious about this with a new carer and very often it's the wife who creates a lot of the anxiety. The only way to deal with this is in a matter of fact, nurse-like fashion.

There are other opportunities during the day to make jokes. On, during and after the commode is not one of them. Jonathan was a very tall man with long, piano-playing fingers. He had very big feet size 13 if I remember correctly and yes everything was in proportion. The first evening after the visit from emergency plumber, never a good start, Jonathan said he needed to use the commode. I managed to transfer him from the wheelchair to the commode no problem.

As is the norm I stepped outside into the hallway to give him a little privacy. He called to say he'd finished. I could empty the commode and then wheel him back into the sitting room to say goodnight to his wife to save transferring to the wheelchair.

The obvious thing was to empty the commode before releasing the breaks.

So I did. The pan slides out from underneath of the commode seat so it can be emptied, washed and replaced.

Although I had looked after men before, somehow I had forgotten about the male anatomy and gravity. Jonathan shrieked like a girl. I was standing behind him at the time. I stopped pulling on the commode pan and peered round at Jonathon.

He had tears in his eyes and he was pointing to his crutch.

Oh my god… I had been dragging his testicles along with the commode pan.

So I slowly pushed the pan forward. By this time of course Jessica had rushed into the bathroom. *What was I doing to her husband?*

I did manage to explain very quickly and profusely apologizing trying to resist the thoughts rushing through my head about dislodged taps and trapped testicles. What a start.

I was fairly sure they realized it was a genuine error on my part and not one of uncaring behaviour, but the next day Jessica called me into the kitchen.

"You know we are happy having you here but Jonathan is just too self-conscious with you helping him with all his personal needs."

I told her I fully understood and started to reiterate my apologies from yesterday.

She assured me this had nothing to do with it.

"He just felt uncomfortable, psychologically rather than physically."

I expected her to say she would ring the agency and ask for a male carer or a more matronly type. But she didn't.

"You obviously like cooking," she said.

I had introduced the subject over scrambled eggs the previous evening.

"So how would you feel if you did a lot of cooking instead?"

I reminded her that cooking was part of the deal as well as looking after them, so it couldn't be instead of.

She agreed but explained that looking after her husband full time had become too much only because it was on top of all the cooking and housework and shopping etc.

"So here's the deal if you'd like it. We have a huge chest freezer and it's only half full. If you would make us some delicious casseroles, homemade fruit pies etc. Chilli con Carne. Anything you think we would like, only probably best to ask me first. You go and do the shopping, the cooking and take over all the housework and I will look after Jonathan. How does that sound?"

She saw my look of relief. I did feel that I had let them down and I did ring the agency and tell them about the new plan.

I have always found honesty is the best policy. I wasn't keen to admit that I had failed in any area of the job description but every situation is different and I was hoping my adaptability would win me more points than walking away from the job.

<u>Outtake. Courtesy of speech recognition.</u>

look of the death Jonathan

…look after Jonathon.

13   A Vision in White.

As a live-in carer, being a light sleeper is an advantage, for the clients. For us however, making a lifetime's habit out of disturbed sleep is not a good idea. Still, first nights are always tricky. New sights, sounds and smells to deal with. This one was no exception.

A lovingly restored Georgian farmhouse in the middle of nowhere, reached by a long gravel drive, you would think it would be the perfect place for a good night's sleep. But there is quiet and then there is, deathly quiet.

My bedroom was on the first floor immediately above the extremely pleasant gentleman I would be looking after. A man of simple needs, he assured me, when I had arrived ten hours earlier. He definitely fell into the needs but doesn't want, category, but he was resigned to the fact. He treated me like a guest rather than a servant. Always a good start.

I flopped down onto a bed that felt like no other and you can imagine how many I have tried. I was later to find out that the bed had been literally been passed down through three generations. It was so comfortable I was afraid my record for hearing a pin drop might be about to be tested.

Mr C had sipped at his cup of Horlicks, starring into the log fire whilst I glanced at the newspaper. Always a treat, as I rarely buy an English paper these days. He had struggled to do the crossword earlier. Not due to any lack of knowledge or aptitude, simply that his sight was so poor that even with his table-top magnifying machine, he screwed up his eyes in a vain hope of making out the words, he could see very little. These days of course, he could have a computer and increase the size of the font on a digital version.

I had offered to read the clues out to him but he politely declined, preferring to do what he could. He wasn't one for television but did like the occasional concert on the radio. This assignment was going to take some getting used to. There was a television, of sorts, in the carer's room. It was a small portable cream coloured Sony. The UK seems to be scattered with them. That and Robert's radios. The ariel sat on the windowsill and could be moved in all directions in the faint hope of picking up a clear signal. And if it was windy, forget it.

Mr C had a very small appetite. Apart from his failing eyesight it soon became clear that his family had quite severely underestimated the state of his health. Either that or they were in denial. Mostly, you are given an up to date picture of the client's health before you arrive. Forewarned, etc.

After all, if a client is winding down, we need to know. Mr C certainly knew, but he never voiced it. If there is one word that applies to so many elderly people I've looked after it is; stoic. I suppose, they are the, keep calm and carry on, generation.

Nowadays, we can barely function if our mobile phone battery dies, let alone a whole human being.

So, that first night I was particularly alert. Difficult when you really need to sleep as well. Mr C assured me he would call if he needed anything. He had a little bell by the side of his bed.

But as I said, he was directly below, so no problem.

I climbed into the wonderfully comfortable double bed. The mattress somehow gave way under my weight, and then realigned itself to support and cradle me. I felt as though I was nesting, is the only way I can describe it. I hadn't bothered to close the curtains on the dormer window and I normally like a really dark bedroom. But somehow this place was different. As I lay my head on the pillow, I realized that the Velux window above my head gave me a better view of a starlit night than I had ever seen before.

I must have drifted off quite quickly because when I awoke with a start I had no idea of the time. I know a sound had woken me but was it Mr C? I couldn't be sure. He had seemed so frail over supper. Cheese and crackers was all he had wanted. And I didn't like the sound of his breathing. I lay very still for a moment longer, marvelling at the stars above my head and dreading getting out of my lovely warm nest. Some condensation had formed on the dormer window and the moon was covered temporarily by a cloud. But it was no good, even though I could hear nothing now, something had woken me. I had to go and check.

As much as I would love to have my big thick dressing gown with me, it is too heavy to carry, so I slipped into my ankle length, thin white cotton terry towelling dressing gown and matching slippers. I didn't bother with the light as I could see quite clearly now that the moon had reappeared from behind a cloud.

I went down the newly built wooden staircase as quietly as I could. No point in waking Mr C if all was well.

Unfortunately the door to his bedroom was of the incredibly creaky variety.

He sat bolt upright almost at once. "Is everything all right?" He asked very politely.

He was blinking hard, trying to make out what stood before him. I was about to retreat with a quick apology, saying it must have been something outside, a fox maybe, when he started to laugh.

He was sitting up and his shoulders were beginning to shudder.

I walked round to the side of the bed so that I was next to him. It was hard to gauge just how much he could see in the semi dark.

"I'm fine. I am so sorry to disturb you. It's just…"

I looked at Mr C who now had his head in his hands. Laughing.

Taking his hands from his eyes he peered at me, leaning slightly over the bed, looking me up and down.

I didn't know quite how to react.

"I'm sorry," he said as he wiped a tear from his left eye. "It was the way you just floated in, dressed all in white. I thought you…"

He started to hiccup through the laughter. "I thought I'd gone to heaven and you were an angel!"

I burst out laughing, although I wasn't sure it was quite that funny.

"Well, I do have my good points, but I'm definitely not an angel. By the way, I did hear something…something."

I apologized again for waking him. He said it was fine and then started to convulse with laughter.

"What?" I had to ask.

"All I did was sneeze…and you were there…"

The hiccups came back with a vengeance and Mr C reached out to his bedside table for a glass of water. I started to move to get it for him but he waived me away.

He calmly took a sip and replaced it on the lace doyley, next to his alarm clock with the giant hands.

"No," he said, regaining his composure. "No, what was so funny was, the last carer didn't even wake up when that mirror," he pointed to the opposite wall, "fell off the wall in the middle of the night, catching the trouser press on the way down and smashing to bits. And you come rushing downstairs like Florence Nightingale, when I sneeze!"

I could certainly see the funny side of that but also couldn't help but wonder about the previous carer…

14   Hove, actually.

However much information you are given you can never be sure exactly who you will find on the other side of the door when you first arrive at a new job. Although described as amazingly spritely for her age, you somehow imagine a lady of 102 must be pretty well, past it.

Mistake number one.

"Have you worked in Hove before?" This was the greeting I received after being ushered into the smallest, most claustrophobic flat I have ever worked in, by a relieved looking, social services carer, who had been waiting for me.

So, apparently, people really did think Hove was something special.

Their mistake. It is not.

The voice with the question was sitting in a dilapidated brown leather armchair that had four, bright orange cushions on it. All of four feet- ten inches, Miss Gloria was not at all how I had imagined. Of course she had wrinkles and grey hair, what there was of it, but no glasses or hearing aids.

I merely nodded at her question. I lied. It seemed the right thing to do.

She pointed to the only other piece of furniture in the room, besides her hospital bed, a rickety dining chair. I sat down, gingerly.

Miss Gloria, so called because she hated her surname, was pointing the remote control of the video player and apparently successfully setting up a recording for that evening.

"Always have to record my evening's viewing on change-over day. New helpers all seem to need to chatter. Chatter, chatter." Miss Gloria kept her eyes focused on the television screen the whole time.

"Can you cook?" she asked.

"I can. I really enjoy cooking."

This had to be a plus point.

"Pity. My friend brings all my food. You can have what you like. Just don't give it to me. Okay?"

"Oh, ok."

However, I didn't get too excited. Whatever you like, may well have to come out of a £50 week budget. And it was after all, Hove, actually. Not cheap.

Mind you, if there was only myself to feed. I wondered where the housekeeping purse was kept? Too soon to ask.

"I'll just go and unpack then. Anything you need at the moment?"

Miss Gloria slowly raised her eyes to mine.

"What could I possibly need?" she glowered at me.

"I'll ring," she picked up a brass bell from the large pocket that hung over the chair, at the side of her. "If I need anything." She smiled a gummy smile.

Only the top dentures were in situ. But more startling was the fact that Miss Gloria was wearing bright red lipstick. Not many clients past ninety tended to use make up, let alone something as vivid at this.

Although she was immobile and therefore vulnerable, I still felt as though she could be a threat, somehow. Weird.

I had spoken to her representative, Sandra, a much younger, old friend of Miss Gloria's. She said she would pop in around tea time, the day I arrived. It was 4.30 p.m, when the doorbell rang.

They really should have swopped places.

Sandra was all, handwringing, nodding, timid and beige.

By the time Sandra left, she literally walked out backwards from the living room, I was convinced that she held some deep dark secret. And that only Miss Gloria was privy to it.

She certainly seemed to have extraordinary power over her.

So there was my challenge for the two weeks. How to find out why Sandra almost curtseyed when she left? Hmmm.

Sandra had left three meals in Tupperwear containers in the fridge. Each labelled with a day of the week. No one can cook like Sandra, as Miss Gloria had already mentioned, so she provided main meals every three days.

I discovered that Sandra was a dental receptionist and worked full time.

She had mentioned her cat, to which Miss Gloria turned up her nose.

"You keep that damn thing out of the kitchen when you are preparing my meals don't you!"

I wondered whether I would get a side glance from Sandra, but no. Definitely scared of the old bat.

"You've known each other quite a while, I take it?"

This was as much as I dare ask on the first day.

"Oh, yes, we used to be neighbours until…"

"Did you say you had unpacked?"

Miss Gloria, giving me the eye.

Hint taken, I retreated to the bedroom.

Sandra called out, twenty minutes later, to say she was leaving and her number was pinned up in the hall above the phone and I was to ring day or night if I had any problems.

I eyed the three flying ducks (going nowhere) and knew exactly how they felt.

"Have you put the oven on? My food does not go in the microwave. That's for your food."

Yep. This was going to be a challenge.

On the positive side it was a warm, damp free flat, hopefully with quiet neighbours.

Sandra came religiously every third day, after work. Miss Gloria treated her like a naughty child. Sandra seemed to behave as if this was normal.

It was certainly an easy job but far from pleasant.

The relief carers would look at me sympathetically. Many would say. Don't know how you do it! She's had so many different ones. No one wants to come back.

That evening Miss Gloria announced that I was lucky to be under tutelage.

"The agency sends me new girls so I can train them up."

Yeah that'll be it, nothing to do with the fact that no one wants to return.

The announcement that I can eat whatever I like turned out to be, as I had feared, an exaggeration. Money wasn't the issue but the fact that the corner kitchen was in fact part of the living room and also housed Miss Gloria's bed.

"Don't you get cooking any of that foreign muck. No garlic, dya hear?"

And you can heat things up in the microwave. Joy.

The oven of course would be big enough for two meals but somehow Miss Gloria was convinced that my 'whatever foreign muck you eat' meal would somehow taint her delicate meals.

Most of the dishes provided by Sandra were casseroles.

Easy on the lack of dentures.

I eventually found out that Miss Gloria and Sandra had worked together at a local primary school but nothing more.

I hadn't long finished reading *Notes on a Scandal*, so I guess my imagination was being fuelled by similar possibilities. But I never did find out.

The day I left, the taxi driver commented as he lifted my case into the boot. He was shaking his head.

"Can't believe they keep finding new people."

Glad I hadn't heard this as I arrived.

"Don't you lot talk to each other?"

Good point. Unless we were actually taking over a client, the other carers never met.

Just think of the information we could share. However, what suits one…etc.

The taxi was pulling up at the railway station when I turned to see Sandra.

She was unlocking the door of a bright blue Audi TT. Who would have thought?

I was going to wave but her attention was taken by an elegant middle aged man, dragging a flight bag behind him. She leant across and opened the passenger door for him.

"12 pound 50, please miss."

"What, oh sorry. Yes here you are."

As I delved into my purse the Audi drove off.

Damn. I like a mystery but this one would never be solved.

15   Just tell him, goodbye.

Only I could take on a cooking job in August. The hottest summer we had had for ages. Have you ever tried to make mayonnaise (no, shop bought, would not do) when you are working in a kitchen that melts ice the moment it hits the work surface? Don't.

But I hadn't been to Devon for a while and a change is as good as a rest.

Again, this placement came by way of a personal recommendation. I must be doing something right.

Tip #9 Never assume.

The remit had also been something that I relished. The job was for two weeks. There would be a two day introduction to all the needs of his Lordship (not sarcasm- a real Lord) and then her Ladyship was going off to Spain with some pals for twelve days. Not the word she used I'm sure but you get the idea.

The part of the challenge that intrigued me was this. Out of the twelve days there was to be six days of English boarding school meals and six days of Cordon Bleu, French style. So, rolly polly pudding and tarte tartin.

I would be given twenty four hours (as soon as I arrived) to write out my proposals for the menus. Then, if approved, I could start making any of the dishes that needed advance preparation.

The first evening I was instructed to make a light fish dish using the ingredients in the fridge and larder. Ready, steady, cook, happily without cameras or an audience. I tend to cook instinctively, which works quite well but I knew I had to get everything perfect so, on the first evening I had Delia with me. The paperback version, which I managed to secrete amongst the folds of the kitchen curtains, in case Modom should wonder in and catch me, cooking by numbers.

His Lordship was a rotund gentleman, prone to wandering into the kitchen, apparently by mistake, as he would just as quickly wander out, without a word. Dinner was normally served at 8 p.m. sharp but as this was August and still a sweltering 28 degrees at 6 p.m., it was suggested that we eat (by we, I mean them, not me) at 8.15pm.

At 7.p.m. I was summonsed into the dining room, where his Lordship was busy, setting the table. A huge oak affair, probably passed down through generations. Must weigh a ton. He was at the far end and didn't look up when I walked in. Her Ladyship, appeared from a side door.

She was one of those effortlessly elegant women that seem to gather in small Devonshire towns. She was model tall, about 5 feet 10 and a size 10. She was wearing the kind of clothes that keep dry cleaners in business. Cream linen trousers with a pale coral coloured silk blouse. Delicate pearl earrings and tan loafers. Her hair was once auburn, I could tell, but was now pale grey and immaculately cut, very short, elfin style.

I didn't hear her first words as I was still mesmerised by his lordship, wearing knee length khaki shorts, a lemon Lacoste cotton tee-shirt, tan loafers (Ah. His and hers, shoes) and white cotton gloves. He was arranging the silver wear. We, I mean they, were having three courses and the necessary cutlery was being positioned. When I say positioned, I really mean that. There was a long, thin wooden stick (pardon my ignorance) which I mistook for a snooker cue, until his Lordship, took hold of one end and used it to measure the distance between the cutlery and the glasses. Oh boy.

Now I knew why some people take photographs. My memory is good when it comes to verbal instructions, but not so hot when it comes to visual details. As it turned out, I needn't have worried. Once Modom was off on her jollies, his Lordship, for want of something better to do, had continued to set the table each evening, with military precision, for himself.

A far cry from the clients who like a TV dinner on a tray in front of the TV.

The reason for my being here was because their usual housekeeper/cook, Beryl, was on her annual holiday for two weeks. Up to Scotland to visit her brother. She had no other family and had been with the Teale family for over ten years. The only other resident of this beautiful thatched cottage was Rosie, the golden retriever. She was Beryl's dog but she was sixteen and I later found out that the gardener, Jeff, and the maintenance man, George (a right double act) were taking bets as to who would go first, his Lordship or the dog.

Apparently his Lordship has a dickey heart but refused to cut down on his cholesterol intake and Rosie was on borrowed time. Great.

Beryl has left me six pages of instructions. Interestingly, four were to do with Rosie, the dog and two about his Lordship's foibles.

The first supper, sorry dinner, went according to plan. The ever reliable but impressive aubergine soufflé as a starter followed by sole meuniere with sauteed garden vegetables and dauphinoise potatoes, followed by rum-soaked baked peaches with mascarpone cream, seemed to hit the spot.

I was just scooping the last of the rum and muscovado sugar syrup from the bottom of the baking dish when Modom appeared in the doorway.

"Excellent. His Lordship is very pleased. He will take his coffee in his study and I will have a green tea..."

"I won't boil the water," I smiled at her.

"Ah. Good. I will be in the drawing room. Thank you."

And that was the last I saw of Modom. Apparently I had passed the test in double quick time and she left the next morning to visit another friend before flying off to sunnier Spain.

Only the destination surprised me. A five bedroom cottage, with stables and outbuildings galore set in five acres. Well, somehow, I thought she would be the Madeira rather than Malaga, type.

With her Ladyship out of the way, his Lordship seemed to have a new spring in his step.

Orange juice, coffee and croissant. His Lordship's breakfast order. To be served in the conservatory, overlooking the pool, between 8 and 8.30a.m.

He would ring the bell in the hall when he was ready.

It was an old fashioned cowbell on a wooden plaque, fixed to the wood panelled hall. There were lots of little quirks about this house, job, people and pets that made this one of my better jobs.

As I was clearing away the breakfast trolley, his Lordship wandered into the laundry room.

"Ah, yes. Out for lunch. Playing golf. Dinner at eight?"

His Lordship never used my name. Whether he couldn't be bothered to remember it or simply thought it was not worth the bother for such a short time, I will never know but he was not rude, just to the point.

"Dinner at eight," I nodded. " Potted shrimp. Rack of lamb, sautéed potatoes and spinach. Creme brulee?"

I soon learned to dispense with any unnecessary words.

He gave me his broadest grin and trotted off in the direction of the four car garage.

Within five minutes I heard the earthy roar of a three litre, British racing green, E type Jag, circa 1975. A beauty. I saw no sign of golf clubs but then I am suspicious by nature.

Once the laundry was sorted, and I do mean laundry, the van came to collect tablecloths, napkins, bed linen etc every Tuesday and then returned on the Friday, perfectly white and starched within an inch of its life. Ready for the next banquet. How the other half live.

Beryl had cleaned all the silver before she left but had left separate instructions on what would need doing whilst she was away. As much as I enjoyed the two weeks, doing this permanently, as Beryl did, made me wonder if I could ever settle in one place.

The words, gilded and cage came to mind.

It was two days after Modom had left and was just 6 p.m. when the phone rang. I let it ring for six rings, as per instructions, then picked up. I assumed his Lordship was otherwise engaged.

"Good evening, the Teale residence."

"Ah, yes..." The line was incredibly crackly. It had felt thundery all day. I'd be glad of the storm if it cleared the air. It was hard to make out who was on the line but Modom had said she would telephone once she arrived in Spain. She was the proud owner of something called a mobile phone. This was 1996. She had shown it to me before she left. It was about the size of a gold bar and weighed about the same. I was impressed. And you can use it abroad? I had asked. So I am told. She had informed me.

As the phone had only rung once in forty eight hours and it had been the fishmonger asking for the weekly order, I assumed it was Modom.

"Hello!"

Yep, sounded like her.

"Is that Lady Teale?"

A voice crackled through the static. So much for mobiles that work abroad.

"I'll just find his Lordship for you. One moment." It seemed like the right thing to say.

"No. No..." crackled the voice. "Just tell him..."

"Any message?" I asked sensing the urgency in her voice.

The signal was lost again, momentarily, then she added, "Just tell him...goodbye."

The line went dead.

Oh, I thought, just tell him...what?

This event was some years before that now famous book, Eats, shoots and leaves or is it, Eats shoots and leaves? But it was a classic example of how punctuation and timing can be crucial.

His Lordship popped his head round the kitchen door at 7.50p.m.

"All tickety boo?"

I gave him the thumbs up, which seemed to startle him so I added. "Yes, right on course."

"Oh and, Lady Teale called."

But he didn't hear me. He had retreated to his study with a large glass of something.

It wasn't until I was serving the rack of lamb and watching the blood pool itself into the reservoir at one end of the silver platter that I considered the message. Just what had her Ladyship said? Was it a bad line? Had the pause been intentional? Just tell him, what? Just tell him goodbye?!

Oh my god. Perhaps she hadn't gone on holiday at all. She was leaving him! Tell him goodbye. No, no. She just meant, tell him (I phoned). Goodbye.

They were both economical with words, so it would make sense.

Ah well, she was due back on the 17th and if she didn't arrive...Beryl would be back and I could leave. I had mulled the brief conversation over in my head so many times that by the time I served the crème brulee I was convinced, she had run away.

His Lordship tapped the sugary crust of one of his favourite deserts.

"Excellent." He said. I was hovering. He seemed to assume I was waiting for his opinion.

I smiled. "Lady Teale called at about six o clock. I offered to come and find you..."

His Lordship continued tapping with the tip of his silver desert spoon, turning his crème brulee, into caramel crazy paving.

"Hmm. What?"

There was nothing wrong with his hearing, just his attention span was very shaky.

"Lady Teale telephoned." I tried again.

He merely nodded. "Any message?"

I hesitated. "It was a very bad line...I don't think so."

It seemed like the safest bet. His Lordship was flipping his sugary shrapnel on its sides, allowing it to dip into the creamy surface below.

I retreated to the kitchen and started to load the dishwasher.

I wasn't sure that he would even miss her as long as he was still fed, regularly.

The morning of the 17th arrived and still no word from the missus. Unless of course she had phoned whilst I was out. I could hardly ask his Lordship. Chit chat was not an acceptable part of daily life around here, except with Jeff and

George, who more than made up for it. They seemed to know everyone's business and more besides.

I took my break as usual from two until four p.m. I was due to leave at five after making sure everything was up to date for Beryl. She had phoned to say she would be back by six but as long as her Ladyship was there I should go as planned. It was 5.15 when Lady Teale appeared at the back door. Alighting from a black cab. I hadn't realised they had them in Devon. It wasn't until sometime later that I worked out she had taken a taxi from Heathrow!

"Everything all right?" Asked her ladyship as she placed her passport and a wallet on the kitchen table.

"Absolutely fine, thank you. Did you have a good holiday?"

She seemed surprised by my question.

"Very good, thank you."

"I'm glad you're back. Were you phoning from your new mobile phone?"

Lady Teale looked doubly puzzled.

"When you phoned just after you arrived in Spain."

"Oh. Yes. Why?"

"It was such a bad line..."

I hesitated. I was overstepping the mark and into 'none of your damn business' territory, but then I decided, what the heck I wasn't likely to come back here.

"When your husband asked if you left a message, I said I wasn't sure."

"I didn't." Getting impatient now. "You've been paid?"

"Oh, yes thank you. It was just that after you phoned I wondered if you were coming back."

Lady Teale stared at me.

"Well, you said tell him goodbye."

I tried to look glum.

At first her mouth began to twitch, then her shoulders lifted slightly.

"You thought I had..." Now she is really laughing. "Do you know I'm not sure he'd even notice as long as his golf clubs were in the boot of the car and he was fed three times a day..."

She starts to hiccup as she waves me off through the back door. A taxi has just pulled up and out steps Beryl. We exchange a few pleasantries, as all the while, Beryl is eyeing Modom, in the kitchen on the phone, howling with laughter about something...

16   Phone your mother.

Tell her, you are getting married next week.

You must be the carer?

Well spotted.

You must be the cleaner?

None of these words were actually uttered, they were merely implied.

"Who is it, Charlene?"

A man's voice echoed from the direction of what I could see was the kitchen.

"You got another new one, Mr P."

She did actually call him that, I am not being secretive.

"Bit younger than your usual lot."

She spoke, tilting her head back and sideways, ignoring me completely.

"Sorry, Charlene. What was that?"

There was a bitter, north easterly wind, whipping along the street and the porch was doing little to shelter me from its grip.

"May I come in?" I managed to say with as much politeness as I could muster.

Charlene refocused and grunted. "Uh?"

Fortunately Mr P had by this time wheeled himself into the hall and was positioned a good five feet behind Charlene.

"Come in, come in, me dear. Charlene, put the kettle on. The poor girl looks frozen."

"She should wear more clothes then..." Under her breath, but loud enough for me to hear.

Charlene, bless her, at least did stand aside and let me in.

Then I saw why Mr P was so far behind her. Charlene turned on the heel of her trainers and headed for the kitchen. She barely avoided colliding with Mr P's wheelchair.

Under the cover of the running water, into the kettle, Mr P leaned forward towards me and whispered. "Been with me donkey's years. Thinks every carer is going to cut her out of my will."

With that Mr P, winks at me at taps his left nostril.

"You drink proper tea, do ya? We aint got no weird, fancy stuff."

Oh Charlene, if ever there was a name that didn't fit...

It was impossible not to rise to it.

"Oh, not to worry, I bring my own. I only drink Earl Grey. Thanks."

Mr P was grinning from ear to ear. He was safely hovering in the doorway of the living room.

I could see his glass display cabinet, full to the brim against the back wall.

He had been an Olympic runner in his youth and now he was in a wheelchair. The majority of the trophies were silver. I suddenly decided not to wind up our mate Charlie, any more. I assumed she cleaned the silver. Not a job I wanted.

"You make your own then!" Charlene spat the words in disgust.

"Okay. " I said trying to sound friendly, ignoring her tone.

I dropped my bags in the hall but not before winking at Mr P and darted into the kitchen.

"Hey, sorry Charlene. I was only kidding. Proper tea will be fine."

I gave her my broadest- we are the workers-smile.

She looked suitably confused.

"Oh, er, okay."

I was sure there was a plant that could use a drink once her back was turned.

"Biscuits! The chocolate ones, Charlene." Mr P called out as he wheeled himself into the living room.

I sauntered back into the hall to retrieve my bags. "Loo upstairs?" I called out to Charlene who was making a big deal out of searching tins, for biscuits, presumably.

"End of the landing, on the right." Mr P called out.

Charlene probably thought it was a pointless question. Where else would it be?

Seeing Charlene's head hidden by a cupboard door, I peered round the living room door and mouthed. What time does she finish?

Mr P held up both hands. Hopefully he meant, ten minutes and not ten o clock. It was 1.50pm.

I hefted my bags upstairs and shook off three of my five layers.

More clothes indeed. I had a job to move as it was.

I heard the front door slam and smiled to myself. Charlene leaving, hopefully. Once a week, the agency said. What was the betting she would find a reason to pop in again before the seven days was up.

I threw my handbag onto the double bed. Yay. I really hate sleeping in a single bed.

And then I looked up at the ceiling. A damp patch, that had obviously been there for some time was spreading. The centre of it had to be eighteen inches across. I wasn't into betting but the chances of some of the plaster dropping onto the bed were at least, very real.

I was aware that Mr P was exclusively living downstairs. He had been ever since he started using the wheelchair. So maybe he didn't even know about the state of the ceiling? I had learnt over the years what one person thinks is absolutely worth mentioning another will totally ignore. The bed was too heavy to move so I was going to have to make do with sleeping on one half of it and hope the plaster did not start to fall.

I would at least hold off saying anything until the next day.

There was a niece who was Mr P's representative. She was due to come tomorrow. I would have a word. Perhaps she hadn't been upstairs for ages either…

I went downstairs to find Mr P grinning from ear to ear.

He pointed to the phone.

"Go on," he said. "Phone your mother. Tell her you are getting married next week."

It seemed that Mr P had been having series of sourpuss's looking after him recently, so I was the best thing sliced bread.

Penelope was an Earl Grey tea drinker. And she was delighted to find someone with 'taste' looking after her Uncle.

"And you knew how to make Welsh rarebit. Many of the carers don't even know what it is."

Penelope had no idea of the state of the carer's room, well, mainly ceiling.

It always amazes me just what people don't say!

I moved into another bedroom. It wasn't much better but at least the ceiling didn't look as if it was about to fall down.

The former Olympic runner was a joy to look after. He was resigned to his fate and was happy to recount his former glory years. He admitted he would rather keep his marbles than his legs. Another lesson in how to adapt to old age.

I went out during Charlene's two hours.

She never likes anyone. Take no notice, was his advice.

Change over day came and another 'new one arrived'. I'd left notes, to let her know that she may not receive the best of welcomes from the cleaning lady.

You can never have too much information.

And, yes, I declined the marriage proposal.

17   I had the bathroom re-tiled after my son shot himself in there.

I always think the first thing you see when you open someone's front door for the first time tells you a lot about how your stay is going to work out.

Coming face to face with, well not quite, it was on top of the armoire facing the front door, a crocodile's head, did not bode well. Its mouth was open with a full set of gnashers. Great.

As it turned out the house was full of dead animals.

The lady of the house, however, was alive…just.

To the right of the crocodile's head was the main staircase. These stairs were only to be used by Lady P. I was to use the back stairs. As you do…at all times.

Lady P was unusual in that she was not very old or very ill, just wanted waiting on, hand, foot and finger. It was what she paid for and so that should have been fine but it wasn't. I had a hard time empathizing with someone whose lifestyle bordered on the adult version of a spoilt child.

It was August in the south of England and I was there for three weeks. Twenty two days to be precise. It rained for twenty days. The extensive grounds, the swimming pool, the tennis courts, all remained, unexplored.

Lady P had a fairly untypical daily routine.

She would have breakfast in bed, on a tray at 9 a.m. I was to enquire as to the nature of this meal at 8.45. a.m.

There were eight bedrooms on the first floor. Lady P's was nearest the top of the main staircase. The back stairs i.e. the ones I was to use were narrow, steep and turned at the bottom, emerging into the scullery, through a walk- in larder and into the kitchen. One afternoon for want of something better to do I timed my journey from the Aga (thank heavens for small mercies) to Lady P's bedroom, via the backstairs and the main staircase. You guessed it. The main staircase was the winner. Plus it was a lot easier to negotiate with a fully laden tray.

This of course was the route I had been forbidden to take.*mental eye roll*

I discovered after more detective work just where the creaky parts of the staircase were. I could get upstairs without being heard. Ooh the thrill.

Breakfast in bed is hardly unusual but a three course dinner every evening?

This was new one on me. Okay, the weather was dire for August but I did find it strange that a relatively healthy, seventy year old woman would insist on having two out of her three meals a day in bed.

I would run her bath at 10.45 a.m and then I was to return at 11.30 to take the warmed bath towel from the towel rail and hold it out for Lady P as she emerged from her bath. It was a small bathroom and she could quite easily reach the towel, with one foot out of the bath. She required certain tasks from me and that was all. No actual conversation was entered into. After three weeks with Lady P I knew only what she had told me when I had first arrived (ghastly) and what that ever reliable source of information, in these country houses, the cleaner, delighted in providing.

At around midday Lady P would appear in the kitchen to discuss the evening meal.

And she would decide if she needed the car to go out for lunch. At this point I would be saying to myself, please go out…please go out. If she stayed in for lunch it would consist of three Ritz crackers, some cheese, a cup of soup (and no not proper soup, one of those instant packet things that taste like hot monosodium glutamate) and half a banana. All the money (apparently) in the world and she eats the same thing every day. Duh?

The worst of it was, if she stayed in I had to join her in her study with the same delicious lunch on a tray. By the second week I used to say I'd had a big breakfast and I wasn't hungry and just drink coffee. Naturally after the morning's exertions she would have lie down after lunch. It was then my free time, to do as I pleased.

So then I had lunch. Usually a salad of some sort. There was an enormous kitchen garden and the gardener would leave enough to feed a vegetarian army by the back door each morning.

On the days that Lady P went out for lunch she would ring George, her handyman/chauffer who lived about a mile away at the end of her drive. When I say chauffeur, he did sometimes take her somewhere but more often than not he was just summonsed to get the car from the garage and drive it round to the front door. She usually rang from the kitchen phone.

There was a door from the kitchen directly out into the courtyard that led to the adjoining garage. Lady P would stand in the hall, tapping her hand on the banister as she waited for her car to appear. George may well be repairing a fence somewhere on the property. George may be in the middle of his lunch but no, rather than take a thirty second walk out of the back door (feel another eye roll coming on) and into the garage, she waits, impatiently for George to do her bidding.

When I had arrived, Lady P had taken the unusual step of showing me round the house herself, even though the full time housekeeper (whom I was temporarily replacing) was still there. Lady P wouldn't let her go until I had been seen, vetted and stamped with possible approval.

Having got over being greeted by the gaping jaws of a crocodile, the piercing eyes of a stuffed hawk and a real bearskin rug I was shown through to the pool room. There was a shower and changing room. Next to it was a cloakroom. Most cloakrooms in English houses do not house coats. It's a posh name for the downstairs loo. Lady P flings the cloakroom door open. It is startlingly white. Completely tiled. It was surprising as most of the house so far had been decorated circa 1945 and had lots of brown, walls and floors.

"We had this completely retiled after my son shot himself in here."

It was said in such a matter of fact way that it seemed impossible to be true.

Lady P's tone was such that she implied that his selfish act had caused an unnecessary decorating bill…

Grief, of course hits people in many ways and that British stiff upper lip, could well be at play here. The cleaner, of course, would have the full story.

I couldn't possibly comment so I didn't.

As handy as it was, I never used the downstairs loo, convincing myself that a run up the backstairs to my bathroom was good exercise, which it was.

When I asked the cleaner about the cloakroom incident, she simply shook her head and told me that Lady P's son had been eighteen when he shot himself and it was never talked about. There were no pictures of him in the house.

"Too painful?" I had suggested

The cleaner, Rosie smiled. "You would think so," she had said. "But no, she just disowned him."

She looked at me as she added. "He never had a funeral."

I asked if there had been a Lord P. Presumably there must have been, at some time.

"Still is," Rosie told me. "He's in the cottage hospital. You know the one in the next village."

"Oh so that's where she goes in the afternoons."

"Doubt it…" Rosie looked as if she suddenly realized she was saying too much.

"Aren't you on your break? Why don't you go out?"

"Been there, done that." I sighed.

"Yeah, you're right, not much going on round here in this weather."

As usual Lady P was back from wherever she went and had left the car outside the front door. She rang George to come and put it in the garage. I vowed at that moment if I ever became seriously rich I would never become that lazy.

By 8 p.m. Lady P was back in bed (her average time out of bed was 9 hours per day, not counting afternoon naps) and ready for her dinner. Not supper, as that would imply a lightish meal. Always three courses and never before 8.15 p.m. Her favourite was avocado and smoked salmon for starters, followed by rack of lamb, sautéed potatoes, baby carrots and green beans. A trifle (homemade) or a fruit crumble and cream for dessert. Lady P had black coffee, sometimes with Bendick's mints. By this time it would be 9.45 p.m. How she managed to sleep after that lot, I don't know.

The next morning there was great excitement. I checked in the household diary. It was lady P's turn to host the bridge ladies.

"We will be using the three tables with green baize cloths and one with the embroidered tablecloth, purchased in Portugal." She announced. Like I would know which one that was? I was to make, yep, cucumber sandwiches, a

Victoria sponge with jam in the middle and some scones, no sultanas. Dried fruit was vulgar. Who knew?

Although I knew there were twelve ladies in the drawing room, all seated around green tables, there was barely a sound. I was just walking through the hall when the phone rang. I placed the silver tray, happy to put it down for a moment, under the ever watchful gaze of Cyril the croc (he seemed a lot less gruesome since I had named him). I listened to the caller.

I tapped lightly on the drawing room door despite being told it wasn't necessary and poked my head round.

"Excuse me Madam but there is an urgent call for you."

It took a moment before Lady P seemed to realize I was talking to her.

"Take a message."

"I'm afraid I can't"

She looked puzzled. *Had she seen me write? Was I illiterate?*

"Who is it?"

What could I say? The truth?

"It's the hospital, madam."

"Tell them I'll phone back."

I wanted to say, which bit of urgent did you not understand?

I bit my lip and I didn't budge.

"Well?" Lady P glanced at her watch. "The tea?"

"Yes, it's here in the hall."

I turned and brought in the tray. I picked up the phone on the way back.

"I'm sorry. I have told Lady P but she said she would phone back."

An impatient voice on the other end said. "Please take the phone to her. We need to know that she has this message."

I could understand what she meant but I didn't fancy interrupting, again.

This time I didn't knock.

"The hospital needs to speak with you."

I tried to keep my sense of irritation out of my voice. Failed.

"I said…" began Lady P. "Oh put it on speaker phone!"

I did as I was told, holding the phone at arm's length.

"Lady P speaking. Who is this?"

"Staff nurse James your Ladyship. Your husband's condition has worsened and we feel we must ask you to come to the hospital."

Lady P was busy pouring Darjeeling into plain white, bone china cups.

"Why?" She directed her voice towards the phone.

"I'm sorry…I'm not sure I understand your question?"

"Why," she gives an exaggerated sigh, "should I come to the hospital? I am playing Bridge you know!"

"I'm afraid it's possible he may not last the night."

"Well there's little point in me coming then."

There was a collective stifled gasp from eleven heads.

Lady P looked at me as if she wondered why I was still there.

I took the handset off speaker phone and went back into the hall, closing the door.

"I am sorry…" I began

"Don't *you* worry. We didn't expect her to come but we had to be sure she knew the situation. I'll have to call again if anything changes. OK?"

"Oh, yes, sure."

I didn't sleep very well that night. I kept expecting the phone to ring. It didn't.

Any number of scenarios were whizzing round my head. Perhaps Lady P 'blamed' her husband for their son's death. Perhaps she just married for the money and had never loved her husband. Maybe her husband was a pig. Maybe her husband had said he didn't want to see her. You usually never get to find out.

The morning after the hospital's call, Lady P was already up and out of bed when I went in to ask what she would like for breakfast.

She informed me that she had to go out and would just have coffee in her study.

Coffee and a couple of cigarettes.

I was intrigued to know if she had managed her bath all on her own…

George had been summonsed and had the car waiting at the front door when I went to the porch to collect the post.

The resident housekeeper was due back that afternoon so I just had to tidy round. No lunch required for lady P.

It was one week later when I got a call on my mobile from the local police station.

They said they were just eliminating me from their enquiries but had to ask if I had seen anything suspicious during the last night of my stay.

I said I hadn't slept well due to pending demise of Lady P's husband. But I hadn't heard or seen anything untoward.

The young (he sounded young) police officer thanked me and said he was sure there was no need to contact me again. Curiosity being my middle name I had to ask…

He surprised me by telling me that Lady P had reported a burglary during the night.

I said I presumed no one had stolen the crocodile's head? He laughed and said not as far as he knew. The items stolen were apparently some fine jewellery.

But I was not considered a suspect.

Always a good thing to hear.

****

I was back in the same village two weeks later and bumped into George.

I mentioned the phone call to him.

He wasn't subtle.

"Insurance scam." He scoffed.

I wasn't entirely surprised. These piles take some looking after. It just always amazes me that so many seem incapable of downsizing and resort to criminal (allegedly) means to keep up appearances.

"The engine was still warm when she called me to bring the car round that morning."

He rolled his eyes, patted me on my shoulder and off he went.

"Oh George, "I called after him. "What about her other half?"

"Oh, he croaked that afternoon but she never went," he called back. "She's got the decorators in now. She's away somewhere. Left Maisie in charge."

"Maisie?"

I was sure that wasn't the housekeeper's name.

"You not met her? She was engaged to Lady P's son. Her and lady P. Like peas in a pod. Wouldn't put anything past them. Look, gotta go. Bye."

With that, I almost wished I hadn't bumped into George. I felt my Miss Marple brain whizzing into action. A dead son. A look-a-like, almost, daughter in law. Missing jewellery and a disowned, now dead husband.

Pity that old croc couldn't talk…

18   We're off home now. Thank you for having us.

I have a theory about Guernsey. I don't think it's real. I think it is some time-continuum, space thing. So many lanes have pavements on one side. Sensible you might say, if the lanes are narrow. And in principle I agree but the one sided pavement doesn't run the length of the street. Oh no. It runs for a few yards then stops and switches to the other side...again and again. So, to walk safely back from the shops, loaded down with shopping bags, i.e. on the pavement you have to keep swopping sides of the street.

Tip #10. Be prepared for anything.

It was safe to go out during the day. Derby and Joan (not their real names) would stick to their routine without problem. Between 2p.m and 4p.m was nap time. Nothing remarkable you might think until you discover that neither of them has a short term memory worth noting. Come 8p.m onwards and it was a very different story. Of paramount importance, the outgoing carer, told me, was to make sure all the doors were deadlocked by 7p.m. If not there could be real problems.

Derby and Joan both suffered from dementia. Interestingly, the one was very clear about the state of the other's mind but not their own.

After a couple days, Joan took me to one side and said. "He's not all there you know. Don't mind anything he says."

I assured her I wouldn't. Soon after, as I was laying the afternoon tea tray on the coffee table in the lounge, and Joan was scurrying down the hall to the powder room, Derby took hold of my arm and said. "She gets very confused these days. Isn't it sad when they go like that?"

I agreed it was sad.

Joan had returned and was about to sit down on the sofa beside her husband of fifty three years, when I noticed her skirt was hitched up at the back, showing her stocking tops. I managed to release the skirt by pretending to help Joan into her seat.

Derby winked at me.

See what I mean? He mouthed at me.

"You know, this wallpaper reminds me of the one we've got at home." Stated Joan.

Both Derby and Joan, tilted their heads to one side as if the patterned wallpaper might please them better at an angle.

"Nah, different colour to ours!" Derby was sure.

"Are you sure?"

Joan winked at me whilst making a circling movement with her right hand pointed at her head.

I had learnt some years before that it is often better to go with the flow in these situations. Pointing out that they were actually in their own home would cause unnecessary conflict.

As it turned out this was the least of my problems.

"Oh go on just let me a have quick feel." This was Derby, 92 and deaf as a post.

This he shouts at me as he chases me round the kitchen table.

"Tell the old fool I can hear him." This was Joan shouting from the other end of the bungalow. Somehow, Derby was convinced that if he can't see his wife of the last sixty nine years then she can't possibly know what he is doing.

I shouted back to reassure Joan that I was managing to outrun 'the old fool'.

"What you saying?"

Derby assumed as we were the only two people in the kitchen I must be talking to him.

"No, Derby, no."

"Ooh, go on. I could be dead tomorrow."

"You probably will be if Joan remembers…"

"Joan, where? I can't see her!"

Fortunately, Derby was soon out of breath and decided he would rather go and play in the garden, anyway.

"I'm going to prune those roses." He said defiantly.

We had had this conversation yesterday. Maybe he remembered.

Rusty secateurs in shaky, diabetic hands. Never a good combination. But trying to stop someone with Alzheimers is often like trying to stop a twenty ton truck. Neigh impossible.

I had rung his daughter. Yes, she informed me. His tetanus was up to date. Let me know if you need help. The daughter lived nearby and was willing to step in if things, got, out of hand.

I had managed to deter Derby, the day before with the promise of shortbread with his coffee and told him it was about to rain. Not a cloud in the sky but Derby was already sitting with his back to the window, holding out his plate.

That was yesterday. Today, he wouldn't be swayed. He was also having a major, albeit temporary sulk. He would soon forget and move onto something new.

I watched as Derby passed the kitchen window clutching a very rusty pairs of shears.

I counted slowly. I got to eight before he reappeared, holding a bloody finger up to the window for my inspection. That didn't take long, I thought to myself.

I had the daughter on speedial.

"Sorry but I think it's going to need stitches."

"I'll come round and don't worry. I know he is impossible to stop at times."

Mabel entered the kitchen from the hallway just as Derby stepped in through the back door.

He was shaking his left hand quite vigorously, spraying blood as he did so,

Joan, of course, screamed.

She seemed incapable of recognising her husband at this point and merely focused on the bleeding finger and not the person attached to it.

Fortunately the doorbell rang and Daphne appeared as if by magic. She always let herself in with her key. Sometimes her parents recognised her sometimes they didn't.

"Is it your day to do the cleaning? You could start with the windows." Joan asks her daughter.

"No, Ma. I'm her to see to dad's finger."

"Oh, you're a nurse, that's nice. I've been having a lot of trouble with my waterworks. You got anything for that?"

Daphne glanced at me.

"You got enough pads?"

"Yes we're fine. You take your dad I'll get us some tea ready. Don't suppose you will be long."

I got Joan settled in front of the television and then went into to my room, for a break. I wouldn't go out today and leave Joan on her own. You have to be flexible with this job.

Some places feel quite homely and you tend to unpack straightaway and others you just live out of your suitcase. More often than not it saves trying to remove that musty old wardrobe smell from your clothes at a later date.

It also has the desired psychological effect of reminding you on a daily basis that this is only temporary.

I opened my suitcase lid to find yet another package. A new nightdress, still in its wrapper. Ah, dear Joan. She kept giving me presents. After discussing this with her daughter we decided it was best to say nothing and just put them back in Joan's wardrobe. Accepting gifts is a no-no, even when the client is compis mentis.

Of course the real problems arise when the client starts to take things away from your room instead of adding them. As a precaution, Daphne decided that a lock should be put on the carer's door. It was soon put to the test when one night Derby 'decided' to sleepwalk. Never the best way to wake up. To see your bedroom door handle, twist, turn and rattle.

I just shouted. "Back to bed Derby, it's only five thirty."

Silly of me really. Time had long since meant anything to either Derby or Joan, although they did have a general body clock. But he went back to his room.

Each evening, as instructed I made sure the front door was secure with the mortice lock and not just the Yale. Most evenings at about eight o-clock, they would nod at me and say. "We must be off now. Thank you for having us."

"We need to get the last ferry home"

"Been very nice. Shall we come again?"

This was the tricky one. Tell them they were already home and there would be ructions.

"This is not our house. Is it Derby?"

Derby would dutifully shake his head.

Then he would look around and say. "Similar…"

Joan would shake her head and smile at me. He's lost his marbles, she wanted to say.

The thing that worked best was to produce two mugs of hot cocoa.

"Can't have you going out without a hot drink inside you!"

This usually worked. Coats would be shrugged off. I would quickly put them back in the hall cupboard (out of sight) and find a nice nature programme on television for them to watch.

"Who's that in our garden?" Joan would often say.

She thought she was looking through their window and not into the tv.

Happily for all concerned both Derby and Joan's dementia stayed manageable for some months to come.

It was fascinating to see how the levels of dementia would vary hour by hour and oscillate between them, rarely were they at the same level at the same time.

19   Short term memory. Nil.

Son Marcus and daughter Jane have the task of telling their father Jim who is suffering from severe dementia that his wife is dead.

Marcus: "Dad. We have some bad news."

Jim looks at them, blank. No reaction.

Jane leans forward in her seat and takes hold of her father's hands.

Jane: "Dad. You know how poorly she was. She's gone. Last night."

Another resident in the nursing home pokes his nose round the door.

Jane: "Hello George."

George: "Hello, don't see you here very often."

Jane and Marcus stare at George.

Marcus: "He doesn't know us George."

George: "What you here for then?"

Jane: "Ma has died."

George: "Mary is dead. When?"

Marcus: "Last night."

Jim: "Who died?"

Marcus: "Mary. Your wife."

He looks from one to the other. No reaction.

Jane and Marcus raise eyebrows at George. He beats a hasty retreat.

Marcus: "We are going to arrange the funeral as quick as we can. We'll come and fetch you on the day... Dad?"

Jane: "It's no good. Let's go."

Another face appears at in the doorway.

Jane: "Oh, hello Matron. George told you?"

Matron: "Yes. I'm so sorry. It's good that you're both here."

Marcus: "Is it?"

Jane: "Dad doesn't know us, does he?"

Matron: "It's unlikely. We can't be a hundred per cent sure. You'll let us know when the funeral is?"

Jim: "Funeral, funeral...Has someone died?"

20   Sherry by street light.

A retired school teacher, nay mistress, that's what she would have been. Schoolmistress, I mean, not the other kind. In fact I had been warned that Miss Pennybridge was of the 'old school'. She likes everything neat and tidy with absolutely no change to her routine or to any of her belongings. This was underlined, twice.

Some carers had previously suggested a slight improvement to her surroundings. All such comments were met with quiet disdain.

The house was huge. It consisted of five bedrooms, three living rooms, an enormous kitchen which led to an old fashioned scullery and a study. The latter being the smallest room, about ten feet square, and is often the case, the room that is used the most.

The house was built in Lutyens style but Jekyll apparently had nothing to do with the garden. It was flat and boring. Miss P had inherited the house from her parents. Her only brother had been killed in the war. There were photos of him in every room. I don't like stereotypes or pigeonholing people but Miss P was the quintessential English spinster. She knew only her immediate neighbours, by know, I mean she would recognise them in a crowd and was on nodding terms, if absolutely necessary.

She had grown up two streets away, went to the local schools, where she later taught and had never left the country. In fact I was later to find out that her only excursions over her 93 years had been on family holidays to Bridlington, east

Yorkshire. She told me this one day, as if confessing some act of infidelity. She had left the borders of Somerset and they allowed her back in...

Miss P had a routine. It never faltered. She told me with fierce pride that she had never been ill, never had a day off school, either as a pupil or teacher. Remarkable. She had a radio, yes, a Robert's (green this time) by the side of her bed which was tuned to radio 4 so that she could listen to the farming news at 6 a.m. Another radio, a small silver Sony, was in the bathroom so that she could listen to the news whilst getting washed and dressed. She always took her clothes into the bathroom with her and locked the door. Miss P wore the same plaid skirt with a variety of cream, pale blue and lemon blouses. Slippers until breakfast and then sensible navy or cream lace ups for the rest of the day.

She was slim to the point of being bony, had a mass of once red hair and her clothes hung around her.

She was not unfriendly but I feared a hug might send her over the edge.

Miss P didn't really require conversation she just wanted someone who would fit in to her routine and preferably make her porridge just the way she liked it. Thin enough to pour and with the top of the milk scooped onto it and woe betide anyone who ran out of Demerara sugar, which she piled on. One morning I forgot the pinch of salt, to be stirred in whilst making. She knew but assured me it wasn't a hanging offence. Not the first time, anyway. Miss P had made a joke…I think.

Her daily routine never faltered. She was obviously comforted by this. I am the polar opposite and struggle to adapt to this way of thinking. I respect other people's routines but for me it's like being trapped in a zoo. Why bother being human, with a whole world out there if you are going to stay in one street and one routine, most of your life.

The only thing that altered was sherry time.

This depended upon the seasons or more accurately, lighting up time.

This particular quirk had been noted by previous carers.

Sherry time is the only thing that ever alters in her strict routine.

She will not under any circumstances have her tipple until the street lights come on.

So that makes a difference of about five hours, winter to summer.

We (previous carers) had all noted how much more relaxed Miss P was after her little drink. This meant if you were there in summer, you could be waiting a long time…

I went in the winter, so we had quite jolly evenings.

That's if you count Scrabble as a source of jollyment.

I had to wonder if any of the others had been tempted to ring the council and say, please, I know it's early but can you put the street lights on in Acaia Avenue? It would make for a more relaxed evening. I guess no one ever did.

21. **Just Winifred**

Winifred, to my mind was nothing short of incredible. She had the most wicked sense of humour and to say we got on like a house on fire was an understatement.

She had been suffering for years with what the Doctor had diagnosed as cystitis which in reality was bladder cancer.

She was in the most terrible pain but never lost her sense of humour.

I arrived on the day before her leaving party.

This gives you some idea of her sense of humour. Not many people will put on a bash inviting family and friends knowing full well, it'll be her last party.

It was October and the medical profession sincerely doubted that she would see Christmas. Winnie survived until the February and I am quite convinced as much as anything just to prove the doctors wrong.

I don't want to give away any great personal details of this incredible woman just share with you one or two really funny moments that I'm pretty sure she would be happy for you to share.

The best way I can describe Winifred would be like a grown up tomboy and she lived in the most wonderful cottage in a village in Shropshire, the like of which I haven't found since.

The sense of camaraderie in that village is worthy of a special note.

There were times when I felt like I was playing out, a fifties, original version of Just William. Only this time it was, Just Winifred.

I had found a kindred spirit.

The first night of my arrival and the day before the party, Win was full of mischief.

I helped her into bed and asked her how much of the liquid morphine she would like?

She had a long eared rabbit not a real one, a stuffed one that resided on her bed.

She got into bed and rabbit went too. He was fondly known as Wabbit with a W.

Winifred and Wabbit. What a combination.

I tucked Winnie in under her duvet and Wabbit too. Winnie immediately pulled out the rabbit's ears outside of the bedclothes explaining that he was too hot with his ears inside.

I nodded, imitating her semi-serious expression and we were mates for life.

The next morning Winifred was getting dressed. She needed some help mainly due to the excruciating pain she was in. She hooked up her bra and held out the right cup. It was empty. She had had a mastectomy ten years previously. I picked up the chicken fillet as she called it and lobbed it across the room where she caught it in her bra cup.

If this doesn't sum up the kind of relationship we quickly formed I don't know what does.

Of course, she wasn't perfect but then who is. She was extremely stubborn and unforgiving. This I ascertained from family and friends. In the end I only knew Winifred for two short months. I didn't stay with her until the end. She went into a hospice for the last month or so of her life. By this time I was living abroad, but I kept in touch.

Some people you just become so close to so quickly. And I may not have been the best person to have around at the end. At least that's what I told myself.

Winifred had a team of district nurses who would come in to attend to her needs beyond my remit as a carer. Injections and so on.

There were four regular nurses, all of whom had completely different characteristics.

And each one of them Winifred could imitate to perfection. Unfortunately she would do this the moment their backs were turned and somehow I had to keep a straight face…

She really was, Just Winifred.

The party went as well as could be expected. Winifred took ghoulish delight in anticipating how people would cope and what they would say to her. Most people managed to behave as if they were at any other party. Of course they had to avoid talking about plans for Christmas and next year because quite frankly that would be taking it too far.

There were one or two tearful goodbyes with Winnie hamming it up saying things like…Now don't forget I want lots of flowers.

She was exhausted but was so glad she had done it. Not so much that it was lovely to see all my friends one last time more a case she enjoyed watching everybody squirm. I'm sure she used to chop up worms in the garden as a child.

I had prepared Win's bedroom as instructed. All the necessary medications, radio, tissues, glass of water, commode, intercom, etcetera by the side of the bed.

Then I began what became a nightly routine of rearranging Wabbit into various positions in fact sometimes… contortions.

I could see Winifred was suffering from mixed emotions but she wanted to continue her naughty schoolgirl façade. It was what kept her going.

So when she came into the bedroom she howled with laughter. I had strung her rabbit up by his ears to the light pulley over the bed so that he dangled above her pillow.

"No!" she screamed. This was a bit unfortunate because some of her family were still in the house. We were both laughing but of course two terrified cousins appeared in the doorway. They had been upstairs and I had forgotten that the monitor come intercom was switched on in my bedroom and so Winifred's scream echoed around the house.

"Look what she's done up to my Wabbit!"

Winnie was laughing and shaking. Demanding the number for RSPCA. The cousins were not amused.

Was I a suitable carer…torturing stuffed animals?

It soon became evident that we were well suited and I hope I managed to find the right balance between sensitivity and completely bonkers behaviour.

Winifred needed strong pain relief but didn't like the way it zonked her out

When Winifred was finally, I can't say laid to rest, because she wanted it to be a natural burial and she chose as she did with every aspect of her life to be different. She was buried in a wood in a wicker coffin *up right*, to save space.

I wrote a poem for Winifred but I didn't go to the funeral.

The one thing I learned from Winifred and her wonderful village commune, the one that supported her through some of her longest days, is that this was what I wanted. She had so much support from family and friends. So many visitors I had to keep a diary and stagger the visiting times so that she wasn't overwhelmed.

The village where she lived and could so easily have seen an original Richmal Crompton growing up with her favourite character.

For instance Winifred could manage a visitor or two in the morning and again in the afternoon.

To save people coming up to the door and ringing the bell and possibly been turned away, we had a system where a notice was strung from the five bar gate at the end of the path that led onto the road.

One side read visitors between two thirty and four and on the flipside it said, no visitors today. Sorry.

It was a great system and reminded me of my school days when I used to leave notes for a friend who lived round the corner. There was a loose stone in the stone wall on the corner of my road and hers so we left notes underneath and waited for a reply. A sixties version of texting.

22. Rose.

Rose became an important part of my life. One that lasted for the best part of two and a half years.

One daughter laughed when she first visited by how quickly her mother had gone from, 'I absolutely do *not* want live-in care' to, calling for the carer if they were out of sight for more than five minutes.

Rose had travelled the world with her husband who had been in the army, so she had an easy adaptability about her.

She was used to meeting strangers, trying new foods and managing to be polite but firm if there was something she didn't like.

She had lived alone after her husband had died but had a much beloved cat and a dog both of whom were great characters.

And on the first night Rose pointed to one of the twin beds and said, 'I sleep there' then she pointed to the floor, 'Gael the dog sleeps there and Brandy the cat sleeps there!' pointing to the other twin bed.

She told me. "I can't sleep without a heartbeat next to me since my husband died."

Rose was diabetic but only needed medication not injections. She really enjoyed her food and needless to say loved chocolate with a passion.

And so began the battle. A little of what you fancy does you good?

But chocolate was banned by her doctor. Debates amongst the family ensued. What to do? Whenever I left the house, Rose would go on a chocolate hunt. Yes it was there. She had lots of visitors who like chocolate biscuits for example.

After a while a compromise was reached. I would leave a small amount of chocolate within easy reach behind the biscuit tin. Thereby giving Rose the idea that she had cleverly discovered without the serious risk of breaking a hip. I had returned home one afternoon to find her three rungs up a ladder.

The family agreed a slight increase in her blood sugar levels was better than broken bones. She was eighty four and she was miserable without her treat.

Rose suffered from the kind of short term memory problems that seem to increase as the day goes on. To have the best possible conversation with her it was advisable to phone before mid- afternoon. Although sometimes I couldn't tell if she really didn't know what was going on around her or she just chose not to. She had a way of switching off. She was one of the, been through the war, got to stay stoic, brigade. This was something I admired at the time. I have become far less convinced over recent years as to just how healthy this is…

However, Rose was a delightful lady to look after and has left me with many happy memories.

One of my favourites was one summer she was watching tennis on television.

I was happily reading the paper and only peered over the top occasionally to respond to Rose's comments on the state of play, until she said more forcefully than usual.

"Look at that. They'll have to do something about that!"

I felt compelled to ask. "About what?"

"Well just look, it's totally unfair."

What I know about tennis you could write on a postage stamp.

I just nodded but obviously more was expected.

"What is Rose?"

"Half the court is dark. They'll have to do something. It's not fair."

It was mid-afternoon and the sun's rays were falling unevenly across the court. I didn't think Rose was joking but sometimes it was hard to tell. I went into the kitchen to check on that evening's meal. When I went back into the living room Rose was looking pleased with herself.

"Did you ring them?"

"Ring who Rose?" I searched my memory bank for friends, family, fishmongers? Who had I forgotten to ring…?

"Well, look someone must have complained, they moved that dark patch. Both players have the same light now."

She folded her arms in triumph. She may not have phoned 'them 'but she was fairly sure that just voicing her complaint out loud must have had the desired effect. The fact that the sun and earth move all by themselves was a piece of information I would keep to myself.

I glanced at Rose wondering if she might wink at me, you never knew.

Only the day before she had received a phone call from an old friend. Well, the woman thought she was an old friend but Rose wasn't so sure.

Sometimes Rose answered the phone and sometimes I did. On this occasion I answered the phone.

"Just a moment I'll see if she's awake."

This was normal procedure. I was standing right next to Rose who was mouthing 'Who is it?' at me.

"May I ask who's calling?"

"Major Denby's wife, Celia."

Rose cocked her head to one side, looking very puzzled. You trying mouthing , Major Denby's wife, Celia, and see what happens!

Rose's top lip curled up in a –who the heck's that-expression?

I wrote the name on a piece of paper.

Rose nodded so I handed her the phone.

"Celia, my dear, how wonderful to hear from you. How are the family?"

Rose nodded as she listened. I was clearing away the Sunday papers which I had managed to spread liberally around the far end of the living room.

I looked up as Rose's voice took on a tone I had come to recognize. She was lying.

"Oh Celia, yes that would have been lovely but I have all the family here at the moment…"

Rose comically waved the receiver around the room as if showing her 'friend' how crowded the room was. (This was long before camera phones)

"Okay. Hands up how many for tea and how many for coffee?" I said to our imaginary guests.

I couldn't resist joining in with the deception.

Rose was listening again.

"Of course do and yes it is best to call beforehand. I often have a rest in the afternoons. See you soon. Bye Celia and love to Reg."

Rose hung up. Unfortunately she had started occasionally putting the receiver down, the wrong way round and therefore not disconnecting the call. This was one of those times.

I couldn't move fast enough.

"Can't stand that woman and Reg…what, Laura? What's the matter?"

I was pointing frantically at the phone. I dashed over and replaced the receiver. As I had feared the line was still open.

I explained to Rose who just laughed and said.

"Good. Maybe she'll take the hint."

This was a rare occurrence. Rose generally was happy to have visitors and she particularly liked children and absolutely adored babies. One incident reminds me just how important motivation is when it comes to our health and well-being.

A friend of mine was en-route to Devon and passing through Somerset. She had a baby of about six months old. Rose had been bedridden for two days. Nothing the doctor could specify, Rose was just feeling tired and more worryingly, had lost her appetite.

I hadn't seen much of my friend Karen since she had her baby, Alexia Lemonie Ray. It's not usual to invite your friends to visit wherever you are working but after two years with Rose I felt part of the family. I had asked Rose if Karen could drop by for a quick cuppa and a chat, during my two hour break. Rose said it was fine.

I had forgotten to mention baby Lexi. I gave Karen a drink and popped upstairs to check on Rose. She was lying on her side looking quite listless. I had taken her a cup of tea. Rose said she really didn't want anything and she would stick with her glass of water.

Just at that moment Lexi started to cry. Nothing too startling, just a whimper, really.

Brandy, the ginger puss, decided to stretch and cocked an ear. Strange sound from below. So she hopped off the bed, Brandy, not Rose and sauntered downstairs.

"If you're sure you don't want…"

I stopped when I saw Rose's expression.

"Was that a baby I heard?" she asked.

"Oh yes, hope you don't mind. My friend Karen's little girl Alexia."

"How old is she?" Rose had rolled onto her back.

"Six months, I think."

Rose was now running her fingers through her hair. I smiled. Interesting…

"Would you like them to pop up?"

I seriously thought she would say no.

"That would be lovely."

I explained to Karen that Rose had been in bed for two days and was beginning to get quite frail. We agreed she would just go and say a quick hello.

The frail old lady was ensconced in her best bed jacket and sitting bolt upright when we walked into the bedroom. What a transformation!

Karen started to speak but Rose's outstretched arms said it all. The colour had come back into Rose's cheeks and even her voice had regained its usual strength.

Wow. Borrow a baby, on prescription. Now there's an idea. Not as daft as it sounds. In recent years the medical profession has recognised the therapeutic value of people's pets. Whatever it takes to make people's lives as happy as possible, as they come to the end, surely is worth the effort.

25. Pets. Brandy, the ginger puss.

Being pretty adaptable with people is a given with this job but pets are another matter.

My first serious encounter with a cat was in the shape of a ginger, female.

When I arrived I declared I preferred dogs to cats but was willing to learn.

The dog, a lively cocker spaniel did a little dance in celebration, the ginger cat stalked off and wasn't seen for the next five hours.

Their owner, Emily, insisted that she had to have them both indoors before nightfall. There were a lot of foxes around and she didn't want to risk any harm coming to her beloved pets.

The dog was a piece of cake. Call and he came. The cat…nowhere to be seen.

It was midsummer and not getting dark until nearly ten o-clock but at nine thirty, Emily started to fret.

Of course I had been all round the garden, calling, Brandy. I assumed that the neighbours must know this was the name of the resident cat and I wasn't an alcoholic sounding desperate.

Emily, reluctantly went to bed with her dog by her side.

At eleven o-clock, I made another attempt to find the feline prankster.

Yep, there she was sitting in the middle of the rose garden. Can cats smile? I swear this one was. She was sitting cat like but if she could have folded her paws, in a defiant manner, she would have. Clamber through the thorns? No chance. She could run a lot faster than I could anyway.

Naturally, Emily was still awake. I told her not to worry and I would leave the cat flap open until Brandy came in. then I would close it so that the kitchen didn't turn into an overnight rendezvous for the locals. An image of the Aristocats, sprang to mind.

"I hate to disturb you but I have a feeling she will come if you call her."

Emily slid out of bed, opened the bedroom window and leaned out.

"Brandy, come in at once!"

Brandy looked up. I stayed out of sight. I heard the cat flap go. I needed to outsmart my new 'friend' so I waited on the landing until she came upstairs. I wasn't going to give her chance to dash back out again.

Brandy stopped at the top of the stairs and gave me a full appraisal.

I gave a conciliatory smile. You win, almost, I attempted to portray.

Emily scolded Brandy, ruffling her ears at the same time.

The dog, Gael, was already snoring.

In most houses, cat and dog food is placed in bowls on the kitchen floor.

In some, when the owners have difficulty reaching down to the floor, cats have their food transferred to waist level. This was one such house. Brandy's food and water was placed on a work surface. Never my favourite thing but you have to adapt…for the duration.

Food was to be provided on a regular basis. Replenished at will. Brandy was one of the grazing variety of pets unlike most dogs, Gael included who get fed once per day.

I am coming back as a cat (pampered sort, naturally) in my next life.

The only trouble was, Brandy's food dish was close to the boiler and as she preferred fresh cooked fish, it didn't stay fresh too long.

The first twenty four hours in a house can be quite a learning curve. Never mind the client, each house has a myriad of foibles. Inevitably the gas meter reader will arrive and you search, under the stairs, in the garage and what used to be the coal house…

With so many new distractions, you can be forgiven for forgetting to replenish the cat's food bowl.

Brandy was not impressed.

It was four o-clock and I was just about to take Gael for her walk. Apparently, Brandy came too. Quite normal, according to Emily. So there I was, with Gael on a lead and Brandy trotting behind. Not one to be left out of anything.

Occasionally Brandy would disappear. I turned round only to find she had zipped into a garden or three then she would reappear ahead of us. This cat was fun. I could suddenly see the appeal.

I got back in time to make the obligatory afternoon cup of tea for my client.

We were sitting, going through the, 'have you been doing this kind of work long?' routine when Brandy came into the sitting room with a bird in her mouth.

The bird was tiny and still flapping furiously.

I leapt up and turned to Emily as I had no idea what to do.

"Brandy, that is very kind of you but we don't want it. Take it back into the garden Now!"

This seemed such a reasonable request but I wasn't sure Brandy would oblige.

Brandy sauntered into the kitchen and deposited the tiny bird behind the cooker.

I wasn't sure if injury or shock made it stay put but I couldn't get at it. Okay, it was small but things that fly around your head are not my thing, unless, it's a Lear Jet and then I'd prefer to be in it.

Brandy was sitting in the middle of the kitchen floor staring at me.

What?

Brandy inclined her head towards the back of the cooker. Small fluttering noises ☹

And back towards the work surface by the boiler.

I was still functioning in a jet-lagged kind of state that comes with a new job and didn't get the connection. Plus, looking back I hadn't realised just what a great communicator this was cat was going to be.

I managed to get the soft mop and poke the bird from the back of the cooker. I had opened every window and door in the hope that it would fly away. It did.

Brandy made no attempt to go after it.

I assured Emily that all was well and we settled down to resume our chat.

I had forgotten the sugar and went back into the kitchen.

Brandy was still in position.

What?

As I walked past the sink I realised I had placed Brandy's food bowl in there to soak. Sticky, fishy smells. Ugh.

Of course. The penny dropped. Brandy was without food.

I quickly cooked up some more whiting, the latest craze in Brandy's culinary world and placed it on the drainer to cool.

Seeing all this, Brandy resumed her head cocking from cooker to worktop.

Could it be? She had brought in a take-away, to remind me that her food bowl had disappeared? The more I got to know Brandy over the next two weeks, the more I was convinced. Yep, she knew exactly how to get her message across.

Still not a huge cat fan, my mind was soon altered. By the end of the first week, Brandy would keep me company, between Emily going to bed and my own bed time.

I did what Emily did and talked to her as if she was a teenager. Brandy never failed to understand, it seemed. As she approached my lap, she would sense my hesitancy as I said, paws but no claws. Seems perfectly reasonable. I'm not into pain.

The first time she forgot and flexed her claws, I tipped her off. She never did it again.

Some evenings she would pretend to be a scarf wrapping herself around my neck. I would side glance her mischievous green eyes. If only she could talk.

We had a ritual. The second night, I found myself talking to Brandy just as Emily did.

"Night, Brandy." I said, giving her a friendly scratch behind the ears.

Then one night, I had been on the phone and went into my bedroom and closed the door. I had closed the catflap and all was well. Brandy would automatically go upstairs to Emily's room.

I was just about to turn out the light when there was a thud on my bedroom door.

I was startled but not fearing the worst I opened the door. Brandy was leaning up against it. Well, well, how could I forget?

I bent down and gave Brandy her usual goodnight routine.

She purred her appreciation and trotted off upstairs.

Since then, most cats, down faze me, but none have been as much fun as Brandy.

24. Rosie the golden retriever.

A loyal friend for over eleven years, Cynthia was nevertheless anxious that when she came out of hospital after her mastectomy that Rosie would jump on the bed, as she always had.

Never underestimate animal's sensitivity. That's what I learned in this case.

Cynthia came home and Rosie sat during the evening at her feet whilst she watched television and later, read her book.

The next morning would be the testing time. Normally Rosie, after going for a short walk to the end of the lane to get the paper, (carer in tow) she would go bounding into Cynthia's room and jump up on the bed, paper dutifully dropped onto her mistress's lap.

I kept Rosie on her lead to prevent this from happening.

We both walked sedately into Cynthia's bedroom.

Rosie did not tug at the lead. She had always gone around to the left side of Cynthia's bed and jumped up. I gave Rosie a fair bit of lead to see what she would do. She went up to the right side of the bed and calmly laid the paper across Cynthia's knees

Cynthia nodded to me and I relinquished the lead.

"What a clever, wonderful girl you are."
I assumed Cynthia was talking to Rosie, so I left them to it.

****

Taking a Boxer Dog into hospital.

A hospital in West Sussex takes the holistic approach.

With his wife in another hospital across the border in East Sussex (don't mention *National* health service, to me. It is so dependent on the boundary lottery. Anyway, my client's surgeon decided that he could at least have his dog in to visit…

What possible germs could a dog bring in? I didn't say…

I know, I know I can see the emotional benefits but…

I had to sneak the dog up the fire escape (Doctor's orders) so we could get access to his bedroom without anyone seeing. Just had to hope the dog would stay quiet.

It all went according to plan and it did the trick in so much as his blood pressure reduced considerably but I'm not convinced by the risk factors, regarding bringing infection into the hospital…

25. Work for a celebrity.

Well, not quite. When the South East agency rang to offer me a job, and mentioned the name, they were quick to add, not the one you know.

It must be strange having a famous name and not being that person.

The name was as well known as Cliff Richard or Elton John but I can't say who it was so let's call him Clifford John. The house had ten bedrooms and was set in forty eight acres on the East Sussex, Kent border. High on a hill. The view was stunning. It was the beginning of October and luckily we were having an Indian summer. That's the one that pops along in lieu of the summer everyone in the UK really needed during the six weeks school holidays.

It was a mile from the electronic gates to the house. The letter box was situated by the gate which meant a mile trek (ok, I'm not much of a walker, so shoot me) every morning to get the newspaper then back again at lunchtime to see if there was any post. And yes, some days I went in the car.

It had been explained to me that Clifford and his wife, of the much younger, used to be his secretary, variety, would only be in residence from Friday evening to Monday morning or even Sunday evening. My job was to keep on top of the cleaning and organize any maintenance that needed doing. I would get my own two bedroom apartment on the second floor, complete with full size kitchen, bathroom and small sitting room.

The only other occupants were two dogs. They were kept outside in kennels which in turn were in a compound about twelve feet square each. A Rottweiler and a Labrador. They were to be walked once a day and fed once a day. The walk in the morning and their food at 5 p.m. The owners would take over the walking duties when in residence. I don't generally have a problem with big dogs somehow I find them more manageable than the small yappy type. The surprising thing was the Labrador seemed more unstable than the Rottweiler.

And then there was the Russian chauffeur. I have to call him Ivan. I can't remember his name. Ivan would sometimes stay over on a Friday evening, if he had driven the happy couple down from London. I say happy but it was hard to tell.

They had an unusual relationship something that can be explained by the fact that she used to be his Secretary. Probably.

Of course I shouldn't have been eavesdropping but sometimes it couldn't be helped.

Occasionally, Rosetta would arrive on a Friday evening and Clifford wouldn't arrive until Saturday morning.

Rosetta would sit in her enormous, fully tiled kitchen, which created a lot of echo.

To put it bluntly, they used to have phone sex.

None of my business of course, but the thing that used to strike me as strange was that Rosetta would be perched on a kitchen stool, all the time looking quite uncomfortable.

He apparently was still in his office in London.

None of this really would be worth mentioning, if it wasn't for the fact that as soon as they got together they seemed to have nothing to say to each other.

It was almost as if they were strangers.

Clifford would always phone ahead to say he was leaving and to give Rosetta his estimated time of arrival.

Usually around sixty minutes, during which time, Rosetta would go into hyper mode.

She may have arrived three hours or twelve hours earlier but it wasn't until he telephoned that she seemed to be suddenly aware of his pending arrival.

I was a teenager in the sixties but my passions were mainly music and fashion I was NEVER tempted by drugs and it wasn't until I had innocently mentioned to a younger friend, one much more streetwise than myself, about Rosette's clumsiness in the bedroom… I seem to be forever hoovering up talcum powder.

Of course now I realize the Hoover was probably worth a fortune.

Every house has its little trademarks in my memory. This one had a courtyard that had to be washed down with a special, sweet smelling disinfectant approximately ten minutes before Clifford's arrival.

Not many people that I have worked for go to the trouble of scenting the courtyard!

Rosetta was wife number four. I later found out she had one or should I say two things in common with wives one to three. I think the polite expression is well endowed. It seemed that Clifford had two passions in life. Greyhounds and boobs. Large ones.

Sadly, Rosetta was the archetypal busty blonde who seemed to think no other 'skills' in life were required. To say she couldn't cook was an understatement. I can understand someone not having a natural flair but even the simplest of recipes managed to appear totally unrecognizable, in her hands. To those of you who remember the television series Butterflies with Wendy Craig; she was that type of cook. Gravy sat in congealed lumps and jellies never set. So my main job for the weekends was to cook. Occasionally Rosetta would offer to help and if nearby, Clifford would shake his head. He would jokingly put his arm around his wife. You don't have a dog and bark yourself, he would quip. She would roar with laughter and he would wink at me in a-I'm not really being a pig- expression.

The first two weekends came and went without a hitch and I managed to resist Ivan's charms with very little difficulty. He resided along the corridor from my self-contained flat in a studio over the garage. This was used very occasionally, if he was on call.

What can I tell you? He just wasn't my type. Plus at the time I was seeing a very energetic young man, Andreas, who was half the size and age of Ivan.

I managed to keep the two well apart. It wasn't until after the third weekend I got a phone call on the Monday morning from the friend who had recommended me for the job in the first place. It was a casual enquiry at first. So how's it going? What's it like?

"Yeah, great. Actually it's a doddle. Why? I mean thanks for the call but you haven't followed up on jobs before…Something wrong?"

"I'm not sure but I heard the last housekeeper was sacked."

"Maybe she couldn't cook?"

"Don't think so. She got the job through an agency. I'll see what I can find out?"

"Oh okay. Thanks Nigel."

It was strange of Nigel to call with such an uninformative message. I didn't know what to make of it but I wasn't going to worry about it. Abigail was due any moment and she was sure to know the gossip. Each Monday, Abby would come along and clean the silver. It was deemed a job outside of the normal housekeeper's duties. No argument from me. I'm not a lonely person but this was a big house to be all alone in. Well, most of the time.

I had Andreas trained to walk the dogs, if he was still with me in the mornings, before he went off to work. Andreas of the, much younger boyfriend, brigade. He lived about ten miles away but was a frequent visitor. Sometimes he arrived at midnight and left at 2 a.m and sometimes he stayed over. I never mentioned his visits to Abby. She was still employed by the Johns and I wasn't sure how his visits would be viewed.

Abby didn't know why the last housekeeper left.

"Beats me. They don't seem to keep their housekeepers for long."

"Now you tell me. It's November already and I was planning to stay here until at least after the New Year."

"Hey look, don't worry. Just do everything they ask and you'll be fine."

Abby rearranged her feet a little further down the Aga. We had a ritual. Coffee, toast. Feet up on the Aga. Gossip. She was paid to work for two hours. We did it between us in one.

I was on a flat rate and glad of the company. As it turned out I would soon be seeing a lot more of Abby.

It was the last weekend in November and Ivan had just dropped Rosetta at the front door. She came scurrying into the kitchen, laden with carrier bags. One contained cookery books. Uh-oh. The previous weekend had seen a particularly awkward moment when as a finale to Sunday lunch I produced a tarte tartin. There were two guests for lunch that day and Rosetta had seemed desperate to fit in with conversation. She had failed miserably. The conversation had been centered on famous Parisian eateries and their recipes.

Ah, magnifique. Clifford had declared. He reached across to the sideboard and grabbed his camera. It was one of those, two handed jobs. Small camera. Massive lens.

Clifford cleared a space in the centre of the table and pointed for me to place the desert there. He took several pictures accompanied by polite applause from the two guests. Rosetta had extricated herself from the table and was ferreting around in the fridge for some cream. As she poured some into a jug, thinking I had forgotten it, Clifford exclaimed in a very, 'Allo'Allo accent. Mais non, *cheri*. I did feel sorry for Rosetta at this point as the two guests barely concealed their amusement. I was really worried that Rosetta may reach for the bottle of Croft's original…I was beginning to fathom how Rosetta's mind worked..

Ah no cream with the apple tart. It should be sherry?

I think this was the beginning of the end.

I could see my job disappearing. She had hired me and she no doubt could find a reason to fire me. I had to admit making hubby laugh at my jokes is never a good idea when wifey (sorry to be patronizing but if the cap fits…) is in earshot. I had been carving the chicken when I had asked. "Clifford, are you a leg or a breast man?"

Foolish of me as Abby had confirmed my suspicions, in the comfort of our Aga chats, that Clifford was not only a breast man but a connoisseur. Rumour had it that he was seriously into soft porn and possibly even generated some of it. He certainly seemed to have a fair bit of camera equipment. Clifford had laughed but not easily as I had thought he would. I had crossed the line. Bugger.

Rosetta has tipped the contents of her carrier bags onto the kitchen table. Amongst the books there was an apron. The apron had a basque printed on it.

An ample bosom peered over the top. Suspenders dangled at the bottom edge of the mid-thigh length apron.

I seriously suspected it was not for me.

"I'm cooking tonight, so you can have the evening off. We will eat in the conservatory. Would you lay the table by the aspidistra, please."

I didn't have the heart to tell her that they didn't have an aspidistra. I had heard the gardener giving her a tour of the newly planted glass extravaganza. The plant in question was a giant fern and I wasn't sure if the gardener meant to be cruel by telling her the wrong name or if he never expected her to believe him. Either way, it had stuck.

"Okay Mrs Johns."

I was supposed to call Clifford by his first name but Rosetta insisted that I use her formal title. All part of her insecurity I imagined. Wives, numbers one to three had lasted an average of four and half years. They were coming up to their fourth anniversary. Rosetta was nervous.

I was torn. If I offered to help her, saying, let me do it but tell him you did it, I was risking her wrath but letting her cook meant disobeying the master's voice.

You are paid to cook. Don't let Rosetta do it. Understood?

This was the first conversation I had had with the boss and now I was stuck.

I wasn't so much worried about keeping them happy as keeping my job. The gardens were beautiful. My morning stroll to cut flowers, when there was so much choice was bliss. It had been so hot at the beginning of October I had taken to doing the housework in my underwear. There was a music system that was wired throughout the house. There were times when I was Aretha Franklin, complete with hoover attachment as microphone. *Respect*…hoover the hall carpet...*that's what it means to me*...dust Napoleon's alabaster bust...R-E-S-P-E-C-T...and then the phone would ring.

"Andreas. Yep, come on over. No haven't got much on..."

The dogs had calmed down and seemed happy in their routine. There was central heating in my flat. So the nights were cosy, with or without Andreas. The dogs didn't even bark now when he arrived, even if it was pitch dark when he appeared. It was all going so well. I didn't even have to do much shopping. Harrods, delivered. I rang my order on a Wednesday morning and they delivered on a Friday afternoon. I was like a kid in a toy shop when the smart young man in a Harrods's uniform rang the back door bell. He would always carry the boxes into the scullery and place them on the draining boards. Strict instructions from Clifford. Do not let anyone beyond the scullery.

It was always a veritable treasure trove. I had placed the order but still delighting in unpacking it. Oysters, caviar, gravlax, rack of lamb, t bone steaks, fresh figs, raspberries and ten different kinds of cheese, including my favourite, Valency. The pyramid shaped goat's milk cheese coated in ash. Heaven. I had introduced this delicacy to the Johns. Fortunately, Clifford was out of ear shot when Rosetta declared.

"Phone Harrods. They have delivered a mouldy cheese. It's all grey."

I managed to convince her it was normal. She couldn't tell if I was joking. A constant problem. I had soon learnt not to joke with her. But how to do deal with the current situation? Clifford was due for dinner at 8 p.m. Timing was not Rosetta's strong point.

But she was determined. She would do dinner. Nothing fancy. A cold starter and desert meant she only had to cook the main course. I left her frantically flicking through a Delia Smith cookery book. Twenty minutes later I ran downstairs as the smoke detector in the hall had started screeching. Just in time to welcome Clifford home for the weekend.

Clifford had brought both the dogs in with him and they went wild in the kitchen.

Whatever method Rosetta had chosen to cook the rack of lamb, it was obviously a tad high.

The aforementioned delicacy was now smoking in the middle of the kitchen floor. The dogs went into a frenzy as they both tried to grab the same end. Brave man that he was, Clifford grabbed the joint from the dogs and hurled it out into the scullery. Rosetta managed to give me an accusing look. Was she going to try and pin this on me? I noticed the saucy apron was curled up in a ball and lying on the work surface. I somehow didn't think Clifford would be fooled. He glanced at me and then back at Rosetta.

"A cold starter and a desert will do fine. We'll eat in the snug, on trays."

This was directed at me. I didn't look at Rosetta.

Clifford played golf all day Saturday and Rosetta had lunch with friends in Tunbridge Wells.

The temperature had cooled considerably both inside and out. Sunday morning dawned bright and clear, with a real nip in the air. I baked croissant and found a new jar of raspberry jam in the enormous larder off the scullery. Freshly squeezed orange juice and a large cafetiere of Jamaican ground coffee and all was well. The tension seemed to have eased…a little.

I served breakfast in the conservatory and asked, how many for lunch?

"I have to get back up to London. Forecast's not good for this evening. I'll leave about eleven. Damn. Where is Ivan? "

Clifford spoke without raising his head out of the paper. We both assumed the last comment didn't require an answer.

Rosetta was obviously as surprised as I was.

"I can drive you darling." She said.

Clifford shuddered as if someone had crawled over his grave. Horrible expression but that's how it seemed. I had never heard Rosetta use any term of endearment apart from during their phone calls and then it had been more, honey bun and snookums.

It appeared she had crossed the line.

A taxi arrived at 11.15 to take Clifford away from wife number four.

I went into the kitchen to find Rosetta on the phone. She was talking in a muffled voice. I could see she was crying. I beat a hasty retreat, grabbing the leftover croissants on the way.

I had an internal phone in my flat. It rang about twenty minutes later. Rosetta sounded strangely cheerful and invited me down to have coffee with her and a friend who was coming over. I peered around the sitting room door to find Abby sitting opposite Rosetta.

"Hey, you're a day early." I quipped.

Abby didn't offer a quick reply. I knew Abby had worked for Rosetta for a long time but I wasn't sure if they were actually friends. We sat politely, talking about Christmas plans and how Rosetta had some of her family coming to stay and they would need extra help. It was a ten bedroom house so I didn't think space would be a problem but I did wonder how many I would be expected to cook for. It all sounded vague. There was a distinct lull in the conversation so I gathered up the tray and headed off to the kitchen to start lunch for two.

I glanced back to say, see you tomorrow, to Abby but she was already leaning forward to hear what Rosetta had to say. Ivan came for Rosetta at 5.30 p.m. She said a cursory goodbye. I guessed she was worried about her marital status.

I was just going to bed about 10.30 pm. no Andreas tonight; he was off in Hastings with his mates, when my phone rang. It was Nigel.

"I found out why the last housekeeper was sacked."

"Oh why, what happened?"

"She was stealing from them."

"Ugh. That's horrible. But what was she stealing?"

I couldn't imagine hauling ornaments, paintings, jewellery, into shops?

"Cash, apparently."

"But there is a housekeeping purse and you have to keep receipts. And in any case most of the stuff is delivered and paid for on account. So how…?"

"There is a safe. With cash and videos."

"There is, where?" I hadn't seen one but then I hadn't been looking.

"Well, anyway, you know me… I wouldn't nick anything except the last croissant."

Nigel laughed and rang off.

Videos in a safe, eh? I started to wonder if wife number four featured in any of them?

The next morning I walked down to the gates to get the paper. I wanted to read in peace before Abby arrived. She usually came about 10 a.m. and left at midday. By 10.30 I was concerned and by 11.00 I was worried and then the phone rang. I dislodged myself from the Aga and picked up the receiver. I was very tempted to say, what time do you call this? Good job I didn't. It was Rosetta.

"Mrs Johns here. I am ringing to give you one week's notice. You can leave on Friday."

I was too shocked to point out that five days was not a week.

"Oh, no, why?"

"I don't have to give you a reason. Just get packed and be out before we arrive on Friday evening. There is a cheque for you, pinned to the pinboard in the kitchen."

It must have been there yesterday but I hadn't been back in to the kitchen.

She hung up. Blimey. Three weeks to Christmas and I had just been made homeless and jobless. And still no sign of Abby. I rang Abby's number.

"Do you have any idea…"

Before I could continue. "Yep, you and me both."

"What, really? She fired you too."

"Yep, yesterday but the bitch wouldn't let me say anything."

I knew Abby had a temper but she was fuming. She was a single mother with two kids. Shit. Just before Christmas.

"Did she give you a reason?

"Nope. Where are you going to go? Your boyfriend's?"

"Who, Andreas? I didn't think you knew about him?"

"I didn't until yesterday."

"You mean Rosetta knew?"

"Oh yes and you hadn't asked permission had you?"

She wasn't accusing, just stating fact.

"Oh shit."

"How long she's given you?"

"Until Friday."

"Christ. Andreas, did you say?"

"Not an option. Still lives with his parents."

That got Abby laughing.

"He has left school I hope?"

"Ha bloody ha."

"Look you can come here, for now. You better start packing. I'd come and help but don't think I'm allowed back."

"But hang on. I get the, me and lover boy bit, but what did you do to get the sack?"

"Honestly don't know. She said she was getting someone reliable, who did as they were instructed, to do everything."

"Weird. Ah well but do you have room for me? With your children…"

"You yes. Your stuff probably not. Some of it will have to go in the garage."

"Okay. Look thanks, Abby and I'm really sorry about your job. Hope it wasn't because of me."

"I don't see how it was but maybe she thought I knew about Andreas. Anyway she won't change her mind and from what you've been telling me she could be out of there herself soon."

Andreas came and helped me pack. Why not? They could hardly sack me twice.

Ivan came down from London on Friday morning especially to take my keys from me and check that everything was in order. I had told Andreas about the last housekeeper and her thieving. But how did they know it was her? He had wanted to know. Well there was only Abby and Ivan and I assumed they were both above suspicion. Or maybe it was Rosetta, setting her up if she wanted to get rid of her. Possible but hardly necessary, I thought.

By Friday evening I had my bare necessities in Abby's spare room. A box room with a single bed. What a come down. I mean I was grateful but… The rest of my stuff, Andreas put into storage at his office.

I suddenly thought to ring Nigel and tell him what had happened.

"I was just about to call you. I found out more about the last housekeeper that was sacked."

"Actually that's me!" I sounded almost pleased.

"You what?"

"Yep, add me to the long list. I'm officially unemployed, oh and homeless. Anyway, go on. You were saying about my predecessor. What happened?"

"You know she was sacked for stealing?"

"Money from the safe. I wonder where it was…did they catch her red handed?"

"As good as…" Nigel started to laugh.

"Why is it funny?"

"I'm not sure you will laugh…"

"Why. What…?"

"They knew she was stealing because they have it on tape."

He paused to regain his composure.

"The whole house was covered with CCTV."

He let out a howl of laughter.

"Oh. My. God."

"Exactly…so come on. Do tell. Just what did you get up to when you were, erm…home alone?"

"Abby!" I shouted. "I think I know why we got the sack…"

;-)

26. Vignettes.

"You will need the iron in the morning."

"Oh okay."

I looked around but couldn't see any laundry.

So I asked. "Isn't all your laundry up to date?"

"Laundry?" he queried.

"No it's for my newspaper. That damned paperboy often creases it."

****

A Dame of the British Empire but what use was it to her when she had had a severe stroke and was unable to communicate. She had no living relatives and all decisions were made through her solicitor.

Looking around at her study there seemed to be as many poetry books as novels.

I thought a little recital might help settle her.

I started to read from Tennyson.

She stared at me for a moment then got up and went into her bedroom, slamming the door.

That'll be a bad idea, then…

***

I started a weekend post looking after a bedridden lady of 96. I was to work (no breaks) Friday evening to Monday morning. It was good pay and seemed perfectly manageable. There was just one thing…

Her only real friend was her neighbour of a similar age. The Monday to Friday carer asked me to sit and asked if the agency had explained the delicate situation with regard to Martha and Bea.

I couldn't recall anything in particular.

"They are more than just friends…"

The weekday carer stared at me as if this would tell me everything I needed to know.

"Oh, I see."

I did.

"And is that a problem?"

"Well it can be if you're not expecting it and you walk in on them in the throes of passion."

I chewed my bottom lip and tried very hard not to smile.

"It's not about disapproving of their way of life, it's just that Bea has a tendency to overpower Martha and she ends up on the floor, then we can't get her up."

Oh my.

It was a busy street and over the space of …hours a lot of people passed the front door. No one knocked. I couldn't decide if I was relieved or disappointed.

***

She was a Yorkshire lass, through and through. To the point, direct. She didn't waste words. She had been widowed for over twenty years. She was ninety two. One night just as I was about to turn out the bedroom light, she said.

"I wish Albert had lived longer."

I perched on the side of the bed, expecting a heart rending account of love's young dream.

"Yes, he's been gone a long time, hasn't he."

"He was good at some things," she smiled.

I wasn't sure I wanted to hear this. Some clients with dementia can become quite explicit with their memories.

I just looked at her until she said.

"If he was here, he could take the bin out, then I wouldn't need you. Goodnight"

With that she yanked the light pully above her bed and rolled over.

****

"Your nephew left in a hurry."

I couldn't think how to broach this subject but I was furious at his behaviour.

I was looking after a very genteel, kind lady. Violet never had a bad word to say about anyone.

I had only been there ten days and her nephew had been twice already. How lovely, you might think. He arrived unannounced and always with a back pack. He gave his aunt the customary peck on the cheek, devoured two large slices of whatever cake was available, slurped his tea and announced his departure.

Violet looked concerned.

"Something you want to tell me?"

She was now smiling.

"It's okay. Well, no, it's not okay but I do know."

"You do?"

"You think something has gone missing?"

I did. I was as sure as I could be. There was a beautiful inlaid silver cigarette box on the landing table. But now it was gone.

I'm not the most observant person but I thought a piece of Onyx had disappeared from the glass cabinet in the dining room, last week.

"Would you like to pass me my portable file from my desk, please? Oh and my calculator"

Curiouser and curiouser.

I did as asked.

"Sad isn't it," she stated. "He's been stealing from me for months."

Violet unfolded her will, flattening the pages on the tray on her lap.

"I've kept a tally. He's going to get quite a shock when he hears my will read. Not only has he been disinherited I have chosen to explain why!"

****

There it was right on cue. The 2 a.m. call.

"Yes, Margaret?"

I tried to do up my dressing gown as I walked into her bedroom. It wasn't cold, it was a cosy flat but it seemed the decent thing to do.

"I want to ring my daughter!"

"Margaret, it's two-o-clock in the morning."

"So?"

"She will be asleep. Is it something I can do for you?"

We had had this conversation over a few nights now and I was beginning to feel the 'repetitive strain to my patience' injury.

I tried a little more forcefully than usual.

"So why do you need to speak to her?"

Nothing. Just Margaret with a pout. One giant sulk for womankind.

The normal routine was to dial Margaret's own number. At least she could see me doing something and then say. No reply. We'll try again in the morning and that usually did the trick.

But not tonight.

"She used to wake me up all the time."

Margaret still sulking.

"When she was a baby. She used to cry and I had to get up."

When she was a baby...

I knew any kind of reasoning was pointless so I just said.

"But she doesn't do it now does she."

Somehow, this seemed to work.

Margaret frowned and said. "I'll ring her in the morning, then."

****

Lenora would sit quite happily reading her book until around 11 a.m.

The fact that she had been on the same page for some time, days in fact, did not trouble her. She had no real short term memory and was fortunately, happily unaware of her situation, or so it seemed.

What she was quite certain about was at coffee time, she had to be wheeled outside so she could wave at the plane passing overhead. It was Concorde and she insisted that her cousin Jeffrey Archer was a passenger and it would be rude of her not to wave.

No harm done. I checked with the family she was not in fact related to Mr Archer. Interesting how the mind works.

Then one day we were watching the news. Big Ben strikes six. Lenora points at the famous clock and says, "I've been up there."

I just nodded and thought. You'd be deafened. The main news item that night was about Jeffrey Archer's imprisonment. Nothing was said. I glanced at Lenora. She showed no signs of recognition.

The next day her daughter came to visit. I was making coffee when I heard Lenora say. "Go outside. What for, dear?"

"Well, Concorde, mother. You always like to wave…"

"What an idea. I most certainly do not!"

So maybe, now that her 'cousin' was in prison she was no longer related?

However, the daughter told me. Yes her mother had taken a party of school children up inside Big Ben.

So you see. Never assume.

****

The Countess of Kirby was completely bonkers. Sorry but she was.

I said I would do a trial week and see if we both survived.

The sad part was that she had a fifty year old son whom she idolized and he was dying of cancer. The Countess was also in poor health but likely to outlive her son. She knew none of this. He was her only light in an otherwise foggy world. He told me he was hoping desperately that she would go first.

She seemed as strong as an Ox, physically. She certainly had Alzheimer's but she had also had lucid moments when she was just downright rude because she was used to people jumping to attention. I surprised her one day when I said I will answer to anything (I didn't expect her to remember my name) but not that.

She had said. "Oi, you."

She never said it again.

The first evening she declared. "See that trunk in the hall. Napoleon left it. He will be calling in for it at the weekend."

Was there more than one Napoleon? The weekend passed, free of small Frenchmen.

The house was in a general state of chaos. Just the way she liked it. Other carers had tried to make a few improvements and been shown the door. None of it was life threatening. I didn't worry.

Despite the enormous memory gaps, the Countess would occasionally reveal glimmers of her former self. On my third night I realized that the system of the Countess tapping the commode legs with her walking stick when she needed help, wasn't working for me.

She could manage the commode on her own and when she got out of bed she naturally banged the commode seat or knocked the legs.

Unnecessary night calls; not my favourite thing.

Over breakfast the next day I suggested she should call out, any name, if she needed help. The idea seemed to take root.

I mentioned it again in the afternoon and again, once she was in bed, as I had become convinced that expression, milking it, was not beyond her capabilities.

It was already 11.30 p.m. and I was hoping for a peaceful night.

It was 5 a.m. when I heard…

"Helloooo. Are you there? Hellooo."

At least my instruction had sunk in.

I popped my head around the Countesses' bedroom door. You never knew what you might find. Details, I'm sure you would rather I omitted. Suffice to say she was convinced it was necessary to monitor the amount of food that left her body compared to the amount that went in…

There she was, sitting bolt upright, her fluffy pink bed jacket tied in a perfect bow and she declared.

"Is that what you wanted me to do?"

She was so pleased with herself I could hardly say anything but, "Yes, perfect."

I left one week later. It was the only house I have ever been in where a Robin had flown in. The house was on three floors and had a central atrium from the middle of the hallway up to the domed, stained glass ceiling. It was impossible to get at the bird. I had heard about the superstition but under the circumstances, a death would hardly be a surprise.

I heard that the Countess died three weeks later, without ever knowing about her son. He lasted just one week after his mother.

And as far as I know, no one fitting Napoleon's description came for the trunk.

***

Some couples, especially the men are just not the lovey, dovey type, especially in public, even if only the family were present. So when my friend's grandmother was brought home from hospital as there was nothing more to be done, naturally all the family gathered round.

Sisters, cousins, grandchildren and the ever grumpy, but he meant well, grandfather. Everyone was making light conversation and generally trying to brighten the mood. Just as the grandmother would have wanted. She was quietly amused by it all.

Then suddenly her husband of sixty three years leant over the bed, with a tear in his eye, and kissed his wife on the mouth.

To which she quickly replied, once he released her.

"Christ, now I know I'm dying."

Always good to have the last laugh.

****

Can there be any thing more important than keep medicines clearly labelled and out of the reach of children? The fact that I was looking after a retired GP meant surely I would have no concerns with such matters. What I hadn't realized was the doctor in question was severely depressed and asked me to lock away her medication as she feared that she could quite easily take a suitable overdose and she didn't want to do that.

I duly hid her medication box. I didn't however deal with the occasional medicines such as laxatives. Like many elderly clients she had a bottle of Lactalose on the kitchen window sill.

She was also a great believer in using Eco products. Can you see where I am going with this…? We had finished supper and I had washed up when I saw the doctor measuring out a dose of her laxative medication. She had her back to me and I wasn't really watching, until she suddenly started to cough and splutter and…blow bubbles!

She had only gone and swallowed 15 ml of Eco washing up liquid.

I looked on for a moment in horror as every time she tried to speak, she frothed…

She rinsed her mouth out thoroughly and we consulted another, much younger, GP friend who said, it wouldn't kill her.

I said nothing but my nostrils kept twitching.

Her daughter visited the next day and I told her what had happened. Her mother was out at the time. The daughter roared with laughter and practically convulsed each time she glanced at the window sill.

"She'll have to better than that if she wants to kill herself!"

****

I can understand how, when the medical profession have made it clear that there is no more they can do, you might as well do whatever the hell you like.

Betty was in this predicament.

She didn't want to go into a hospice for one good reason.

They wouldn't let her smoke.

She had emphysema and needed oxygen most of the day and some of the night.

She had an oxygen cylinder on wheels. It went wherever she went. It was a sod to get into the car. She still went to play bridge with friends and tried as much as possible to continue as normal until the bitter end as she put it.

Her doctor said she could go at any time. They had to be realistic. I never asked the obvious question. Why hadn't she given up smoking? I guessed she must have tried and she must be sick of people's advice, especially now it was too late.

She refused her tablets the one morning.

"What's the point?" she said.

I said they kept her ticking over.

She quite understandably said.

"I don't want to tick over I want to go back to normal or go out with a bang".

Betty had almost had her wish.

When I arrived her doctor had explained how Betty's oxygen mask had been fitted with an anti-blow back device. Hmm. A lighted cigarette and oxygen. Great.

Yep, Betty had nearly got her wish a few weeks back. She insisted, even when needing her oxygen mask on, having a cigarette at the same time. Alternately. That time she only lost her eyebrows…

There comes a time in everyone's life when you have to go with their wishes or at least find a compromise. Betty died the week after I left, in her sleep, with a cigarette between her fingers. Stubborn to the end.

***

"I'm really sorry but the doctor thinks it would be best if you could come."

"Really. What now?" Incredulous.

"Well, he can't be sure but it really is only a matter of days now."

"Can't it wait until after Christmas?"

Silly me. Was it Christmas.? So that's why there was a decorated tree in the house with two presents underneath.

This was the daughter I was talking to. Her mother was dying. Very inconvenient.

"Has she been asking for anyone?"

Anyone but you, you hope. I thought.

"No, she hasn't. She has been sleeping a lot."

"Oh that's alright then. I'll ring you later but I'll have to see. Just bought a new Volvo automatic. Have you any idea how much petrol it uses to come down from Norfolk?"

Well no actually, I didn't.

There was a son and he lived five miles away but the daughter in law didn't get on with her mother in law. They had however condescended to have us over for Christmas day lunch.

"We'll pick you both up at midday on our way back from church. Can you have her downstairs by then?"

This had been the son's instructions the day before.

I explained that his mother had quite simply refused to get out of bed. That's when I had called the doctor. He told me. She's given up. Just try and keep her fluids up. This was Christmas eve. I had updated the son and daughter. Neither was interested. I've learned that you can't judge these situations. Who knows what may have gone on in the past?

Christmas morning arrived and a neighbour popped in. She went upstairs but came down after ten minutes. I feared the worst. The neighbour agreed. She's not long for this world.

I rang the son and explained that his mother needed him to visit not the other way round. They were after all, going to pick us up at midday.

"Oh we won't bother then." He said simply. "Have a nice day."

Was he kidding?

It seemed to have escaped their notice but I had been invited to eat with them as well.

Would they pop in with a plate for me…?

Of course, as you always have to, with these jobs I had a contingency plan.

A chicken portion and vegetables but my heart wasn't in it.

It all seemed so sad that for whatever reason, this lady was alone and dying at Christmas.

It was about 5 p.m. when two grandchildren turned up. They went in quickly to see their grandmother. She raised herself up on her elbows and I took the chance to get some fresh pillowcases and make her drink some water. She was getting dehydrated.

She died five days later but I'm sure the funeral wouldn't have interfered with New Year's plans and maybe they could get the train if it compared favourably with the price of petrol for the Volvo.

****

New appliances of the personal kind often take some getting used to.

Hearing aids are classic. They don't fit, they make your ears itch, they whistle…it goes on and on.

So when Peggy called me into the living room, I wasn't surprised.

"Damn thing doesn't work!" she hollered.

A common mistake. It's not me who's deaf…

"Well, we better find a way because you know the nice young lady who lives upstairs?"

Peggy nods.

"Do you remember, she's a nurse and she's on nights this week, so she will be trying to sleep about now."

It was Saturday afternoon and Peggy was watching the rugby. She was a fanatic. I couldn't really ask her not to shout out but we could adjust the television to a decent level.

"So what doesn't work, Peggy?"

"This new fangled hearing aid. Look, it doesn't work!"

This was one of those times when even though I knew I shouldn't. I burst out laughing.

Peggy was holding the hearing aid in the palm of her hand and pointing it at the tv.

"It goes in your ear, Peg. Like this."

I placed the hearing aid in its rightful place and returned the volume to normal.

I looked up at the ceiling. I'm sure I heard a sigh of relief.

***

It has to be one of the most fascinating jobs, living in other people's homes and at times a truly rewarding job. Helping people to stay in their own homes, living out their last days, the best they can. And it's good to know, unlike a nanny, you don't have to worry how they are going to turn out when you leave ;-)

***

With special thanks to Laura who has now retired but assures me she still has more stories to tell…If she can find the time.

Helen Ducal

Philosophy: The only life worth living is the one you create for yourself.

Contact the author: www.helenducal.com

Or find her on Facebook.

And @Khamaileon on twitter.

Printed in Poland
by Amazon Fulfillment
Poland Sp. z o.o., Wrocław